M000031609

If AND Only If

Experience College in Her Running Shoes

C.S. MCKINNEY

Illustrated by S.L. McKinney

This book is a work of fiction. Names, characters, businesses, events, places, and incidents are products of the author's imagination or are used fictitiously. Any resemblance to actual persons, living or dead, or actual events or locales is entirely coincidental. All medical and other references are fictious in nature and should not be taken as facts or advice.

Text copyright © 2019 by C.S. McKinney.

Illustrations copyright © 2019 by S.L. McKinney.

First Edition

All rights reserved. No whole or part of this publication may be reproduced, or stored, or transmitted in any form or by any means, electronic, mechanical, photocopying, recording, future means, or otherwise, without written permission of the author.

For more information please visit www.csmckinney.com

ISBN: 978-1-09830-977-0

eBook ISBN: 978-1-09830-351-8

This book is dedicated to my father and my mother.

Without them together, I would not be so blessed.

CHAPTER 1:

Sarah

The rain beating upon Sarah's window broke the silence of the room. Interrupting her dream, the noise drew her from a tantalizing sleep. She hadn't slept so soundly in months. As the pattering drops grew louder, Sarah rolled over on her side and opened her eyes. Feeling the monthly cramps, she knew it would be another one of those days. A shower and change would be the first things before getting ready for class.

Sliding her legs over the flannel sheets, Sarah Olivia felt her way to the edge of the bed and placed her feet on the soft rug below. The brown strains of hair fell toward the top of her shoulders, almost the right length to cover her neck and meet the seam of her T-shirt. Sarah shut the door to the bathroom behind her and slowly shed the flannel boxers, revealing her firm legs that stretched to her slender waist. The purple panties were the usual, in case of a leak. Clasping at the hem, Sarah pulled the oversized shirt over her head, unveiling her plump breasts. She had never slept in a bra. The thought of being confined by such support seemed unnecessary.

Being free and comfortable was the most gratifying feeling, even if it was just at night. Sarah stood in front of the mirror for some time admiring her body, legs like spun silk, matched with petite hips and ample breasts. However, the reflection she saw in the mirror had changed, in a way that only she knew. Turning the shower handle, she tested the water before stepping inside and drawing the curtain behind her.

After refreshing herself, Sarah slipped into some dark red undies and a pair of fitting jeans. Finally, she strapped on a bra with a cami and long-sleeve blouse. She peered again into the mirror. She felt cute. Of course, she needed to feel satisfied and confident. The rest of the week was going to be a painful few days. Before creeping out the door, Sarah poured a cup of coffee and popped two aspirins. The first day of the semester was here, and hopefully a new start. Putting on her jacket, Sarah opened the door and quietly stepped out into the rain ....

CHAPTER 2:

If

The chirping birds outside Sarah's window woke her from her dreams. With ease, she leapt out of bed. Anxious for the first day of senior year, she wanted to look her best. After a short shower, Sarah wrapped a towel around her chest and went over to the drawers in front of her bed to find some underwear. She pulled out a baby-blue bra and pair of flowery panties that gave her the cuteness she desired. After slipping on her garments, she removed the towel. A white skirt and a yellow shirt hung on the closet door; she had bought the outfit last week just for the occasion. Once dressed, she slid the strap of her new pink purse over her shoulder. The recent addition to her bag collection was covered with white figures that resembled dandelions.

Before heading out the door, she picked up her notebook and keys, taking a final look in the mirror. She did not need to bother with makeup or fixing her hair, as she was naturally beautiful, and her hair needed no straightener.

The college was only a short drive from Sarah's apartment. Even so, the sun was bright, warm, and welcoming, so she decided to roll the windows down on her vintage pearl-white Volkswagen. On campus, the quad was full of both new and returning students soaking in the morning rays of sunshine. A smile crept across her face as she pulled into her parking spot.

After stepping out of her car, Sarah pulled her bag from the back seat. Her first class of the semester was abstract algebra. Luckily, Boyd Hall was only a short walk from the east parking lot. Sarah grinned to herself, excited for the next four months.

The even flow of students moved fluidly about the sidewalks, streets, and heart of Yemington. As Sarah entered Room 317 of Boyd, she spotted the perfect seat. She liked to sit on the right side of the room, near the front but not in the first row. She recognized a few of the faces, but unfortunately, none of her close friends was in the class. She leaned over to her bag to pull out her pencil, notebook, and water. Sitting back up, she noticed an unfamiliar face filling the door. The young man was medium-height, fit, and not bad looking, but with no further acknowledgment, Sarah turned back to the front of the room and opened her bottle.

"Hi. Do you mind if I sit here?"

"No, not at all," replied Sarah.

"I'm Nigel Branan by the way; just transferred here." He had a bright smile about him, the kind that most women would melt over.

"Welcome. I'm Sarah Mills."

Nothing else could be said, for at that time, Dr. Harvey entered the room. "Good morning class and welcome back." He was probably one of the greatest math professors at the university. His wits proved most astounding, while his humor was greatly loved.

"Today, we are going to start with a recap of proofs," he said. "I know summer has taken its toll on everyone so it will do us some good. Besides, I'm still half asleep and my brain is melted from lying on the beach, so I need a review.

"First, let's talk about conditional statements. If. If is such a powerful expression. It is the beginning of a condition, something that will describe an effect. If–then is even more meaningful. Given one instance occurs, the outcome will be the following. There are no two ways about it, just a hypothesis and a conclusion.

"There are three situations that you should be familiar with. The first is the trivial if–then statement. If you study all week, then you will pass the test. Sometimes, this condition turns out to be true, and other times it is false. This dilemma can also be written in reverse. In this direction, the new statement is what we call the converse. The converse, like the original, can be false or it can still prove true. If you pass the test, then you studied all week.

"Now, consider if these two statements are combined, then we have formed a biconditional statement. For a different example, let's take the topic of relationships. Say we have a young couple that is thought to be deeply and madly in love. Well, we can say the love is mutual by using a biconditional statement: He loves her if and only if she loves him. There is a special piece to this conundrum. Biconditional statements serve a unique purpose and, therefore, are given a fitting mathematical shorthand in which to be written, IFF.

"So how is this beneficial in mathematics? Well if–then statements are one of the most powerful lines of reason. They afford us the opportunity to organize data into sets and then categorize these sets. Math depends on these properties for rules to be established, which support the fundamentals and darkest crevices of the calculus. Everything you do in a math class will be based on proofs that were previously divulged. This class will just be where you begin to write and cypher out such scenarios."

Sarah could feel her hand tighten around the edge of her pencil. Writing was always a fun task to remaster after taking a summer off from classes. The penmanship always looked foreign and the flow of the pencil across the paper felt unnatural. When Sarah looked back up at the board, Dr. Harvey had already switched to blue chalk, filled the first, and was starting on the second board.

"Okay, class, answer me this. If you have the set of complex numbers, how many different subsets of numbers can we derive?" Every pencil in the room stopped, while confused glances were exchanged.

"Ha! That will be our next topic of discussion." Around the room, heads shook with amusement. They all knew he had an odd sense of humor; it just showed up at the most awkward and unexpected times.

At that point, Nigel raised his hand, "There would be infinitely many subsets in the set C of complex numbers."

Dr. Harvey stood for a second with an inquisitive look. He already knew the answer, but he was unsure to whom the unfamiliar face belonged. "Okay…" he stalled, checking over his list of names for standouts. "Mr. Branan. How do you explain your reasoning here?"

"Dr. Harvey, if we can assume that any one singular number is indeed a subset of the complex numbers, and there are in fact infinitely many numbers that exist, then we could use induction to prove this. Furthermore, this same principle would work for natural, integer, and real numbers."

"Very good, Nigel. Alright class, next week you all are to prepare a report on the history of complex numbers." A loud groan filled the room. "Joking. I am only joking.

"I do want to talk about one other piece though. We have covered statements and sets, but what about axioms? What are we going to establish as our base in this class? Ideally, I could make you prove every single concept you use; however, if I did that, we would be here for the remainder of time," he laughed. "To simplify the reality of this class, we will set the ground rules. Every proof we cover, or anything that was taught in the proof's curriculum prior to this semester, will be considered common knowledge for our math community. Therefore, those statements do not need deriving again and are free for everyone to use without explanation."

Once class ended, Sarah gathered her books and notes before heading out the door. The long hallway led out to an oval common area centered on a spiraling staircase. It was 10:15 a.m. by this point, leaving enough of a break to stop by the dining hall for a quick breakfast before going to her next class. By the time she made it down the stairs and to the main entrance, her roommate, Emily, was coming up the sidewalk toward the biology department.

Emily instantly struck up a conversation about her back-to-back classes from eight until eleven thirty. "At least I will be done for the day." Sarah knew how much Emily enjoyed sleeping in, so her frustration toward early mornings was a bit amusing. Emily soon began to joke about a guy leaving midway through her first class after realizing he was in the wrong lecture. Her entertaining morning carried on as the two climbed up the hill to the Biological and Chemistry Studies Building. It was not until after they split off and Sarah was taking her notebook out in the next class that her stomach let out a loud growl. She dug around in her purse searching for a snack that might be hiding within the bottom corners. Trying to put the dining commons out of her mind, she soon settled on a piece of peppermint gum.

Entering with a stack of notes in hand, the professor started class promptly, heedless of any latecomers. As the professor moved from her opening remarks into the lecture, Sarah soon lost her appetite anyway. Ecology was filled with discussions involving the interactions at the different levels of the trophic pyramid. For the start of the semester, Professor Donaldson had prepared a short slideshow filled with macroinvertebrates. Her explanation of how they would learn about and use these specimens for their first lab was intriguing; yet, Sarah had no interest in thinking about eating while viewing a leech attached to a rather pale stomach.

Cutting the lights back on at the conclusion of the presentation, everyone let out a groan. The professor was already handing out sheets with organism diagrams, which they would be required to learn for a quiz.

Sarah first fell in love with biology in high school, about the same time she realized her passion for math. When it came time to pick a college major, she decided to go the math route. However, still intrigued, she signed up for an introductory biology class to satisfy her science core. After that first semester, she went back to her counselor to set up a double major plan of study. She was not sure where this would lead her, but the decision felt not only right but also satisfying.

As Dr. Donaldson squeezed every minute out of the period, the overflowing dining hall came as no surprise when Sarah made her way to the swinging glass doors. Across the way, she could see Emily. She had beaten the chaos or wiggled her way through everyone because Emily was already getting her drink and heading toward a table.

Lunch was always spent talking about their day, watching everyone wander in through the doors, and seeing whom else they knew. Forgoing the long lines, Sarah headed to the fruit and salad bar station to throw together a salad with sliced strawberries on top and a banana for a side.

Emily's eyes grazed up at Sarah's plate as she paused to chew. "Is that all you are going to eat, Sar?"

"Yeah, I don't want to eat too much before practice, and I'd rather not stand in those lines." Emily shook her head as she took a rather larger bite of her chicken.

Unlike Sarah, Emily could eat anything she wanted, not gain an ounce, and run on a full stomach. She must have had a steel gut, because nothing seemed to bother her. Once she ran a chocolate milk mile, chugging one glass of milk after each quarter mile. She not only beat all the girls, and most of the guys, but was also the only person not bent over sick on the side of the track. From that point on, Emily Marie Ellis's nickname at school changed rightfully from Eme to Emm.

"I can drive out to practice today, Emm."

"Okay, that works. I have to go back to the lab after lunch to help setup some testing, but can you pick me up there?"

"Of course."

"I want to swing by the library first and then I will head up." Sarah wanted to check if one of the books she wanted to read had been returned over the summer.

Over the past few years, Sarah found venturing through a book for entertainment quite pleasant; however, she had not always been a great reader. In fact, as a kid, she struggled to keep up with book report assignments. It was not until one year at running camp when the coach lent her a running classic that she realized reading could be an enjoyable way to pass the time. That book was written in journal-entry style, something she would previously have deemed boring. However, it was so well written, she had not been able to put down the book until closing the back cover.

After a vain effort to find the new book and close to an hour wasted, Sarah checked her watch. It was twenty minutes past one, meaning time for practice. Today, the team was instructed to meet at Dever's Creek. After ducking into her car to change, Sarah picked up Emily and drove out to the isolated mountain trail.

Dever's was a fifteen-minute drive from campus, but no one ever seemed to mind. The road wandered endlessly through the mountains, but the majestic hills made every worry seem to disappear. Some people found serenity in the vast city lights in the urban landscape, but to Sarah, nothing was more eye catching than God's masterpiece of natural landscapes, sounds, and radiance. From the past years of being on the team, going to Dever's was always her favorite. It meant two things: a beautiful view and a promise of a grueling workout to follow.

Running had always held a certain place in Sarah's life, but competition had never dawned on her until she failed to make the high school soccer team. Tryouts showed promise in her mind; she had made some notable plays, scored a few goals, and made an uncharacteristic steal. However, when she was stacked up against the top players that made the cut, she went unnoticed. After that, she haphazardly fell into running. Even in soccer, she was always the fastest runner out of the bunch, so transitioning to cross-country made sense. This time, there would be no tryouts; either run fast enough, or end up on junior varsity. Time was the only factor that mattered.

Pulling into the parking lot, Sarah noticed that everyone, except the coach, was already there. As Sarah and Emily stepped out of the car, Emily shed her top, tossing it on the passenger seat. To Emily, running was natural in a sports bra. Trying to put in the time with a shirt on was pure torture and foolish. The guys always went shirtless, so no one ever saw this as being an issue. The team was like an extended family, so formality was not an issue.

Unfortunately, this relationship had not always existed. The first cross-country season was much different. The girls trained and conversed only between themselves, while the guys stayed in their own pack. Occasionally on long days, guys and girls ran together if they had to make up a Sunday practice. However, not until track came around did this barrier break down. Sarah could not figure out what changed, but for one reason or another, the team finally unified as a group. She always thought they became stronger that spring semester because running was fun again instead of being just a constant grinding.

The two girls joined their teammates gathered around Paul's truck near the entrance. Paul was the star runner for Yemington, an All-American and a stallion; but this was hard to tell just from looking. He had the stature of a wide receiver, eyes of ocean blue, and dreamy, curly locks of hair. Sarah had a secret crush on Paul ever since she had met him. Sure, Sarah had told Emily, but gaining the courage to pursue anything terrified her. Fearing that Emily would approach Paul on her behalf, she eventually played her feelings off.

One night last year, as Emily and Sarah sat up late talking Sarah admitted the draw she felt toward Paul. She went as far as saying how nervous she was around him. Seeing the wheels turning in Emily's head, Sarah quickly turned to point out any flaws. "He is too tall for me anyways; we would look awkward together."

"Sarah, you are just picky, but I'm not going to say anything." After that night, Sarah and Emily's conversations continued, but she always wavered from the touchy subject.

"Hey there, girls," bellowed Paul upon seeing the two joining the crowd. Sarah offered a smile, while Emily completely ignored the gesture.

Everyone was in full conversation discussing their lives since running camp; how many miles they had put in and watching the Los Angeles

Olympics. The chatter died down only a few minutes later as a silver truck rolled into the parking lot.

Coach Cavlere was a middle-aged man who once ran in the U.S. Olympic Trials. In his day, Jack Cavlere took the mile in 3:57.5 while he was at Mizzou. There were many theories as to what happened after that, but he had never shared with the team his mysterious past or about why he never qualified for the Olympics. There was speculation about injuries, but others claimed he mentally lost his edge during a race. No matter the reason, his hard-heeled persona and demand for high expectations made no room for questioning his past.

Coach was all business up front, only personable once he knew you were willing to strain your guts for him. While he was always willing to listen and offer advice, Sarah had seen him make other girls cry, girls who had been star runners but came up short on race day. To Coach, each race was a new evaluation. He cared little about what someone did two weeks ago, as regionals and nationals were at his sole focus. He trained you to PR at the end of the season, which most everyone did. Nothing less was expected.

"Everyone gather around! We have much to do this season. Last year, as you may recall, we missed sending both our teams to nationals by only a few points. Today, we are going to continue our journey in search for two regional titles. That said—"

A midnight blue crotch rocket buzzing up to the crowd cut his speech short as the bike stopped along the edge of the grass. The man slowly stood up and kicked the stand into place. Once he removed his helmet, Sarah recognized the imposing figure.

"… Umm… excuse me…" barked Cavlere.

"My apologies. I'm Nigel; just transferred here from up north. I was hoping to catch you sooner before you left the school, but I ended up getting directions from the Athletic Department. Any chance I can try out for the team?"

"We do not have tryouts; our team is pretty stacked from our returning underclassmen. However, if you can pull your own, we always welcome inner competition."

"Like I was saying," Cavlere continued. "We are going to start the season out right with mile repeats. For those of you who improperly train over the summer and cannot handle the workout, we will see you next season when you get your life together." Everyone knew this remark was namely pointed at Nigel, for they were all ready for a speed day after coming off a summer loaded with distance.

"I want a ten-minute warm up at minimum from you all. You know the rule, if you are not sweating before you step up to the starting line, then you are not racing, or, in this case, practicing. I cannot afford having athletes getting hurt the first week of practice from pure laziness." As Coach was finishing his lecture, Sarah took a few hair clips and fastened her hair back into a bun, leaving a few whimsical bangs and the rest mainly behind her ears.

The sun was beaming down on the runners as they circled around the gravel track. Sarah and Emily were leading the girls' team. Emily never overtook Sarah but was always close enough to push each other. "5:51!" he bellowed as they crossed the line. "Remember girls, negative splits!" yelled Coach Cavlere. They were slowly widening the gap that separated themselves from the other girls. "5:55 ladies! Two minutes off; then you're back on. Keep moving around until time to start again."

While Sarah and Emily were jogging during their rest, Emily noticed something quite peculiar. "Look, Sar," she whispered. On the line, ready for the first heat of the guys' second mile crouched Paul and Nigel.

"Okay boys, I want to see at least one second better than your 5:15." The two girls were somewhat shocked at what they heard. Paul was a senior, but the entire last year he had been the top male, always at least ten seconds ahead of the others in each race.

By the time Sarah and Emily had finished their second repeat in 5:49, the guys were on their third lap. Nigel and Paul were stride for stride. Sarah knew this had to be killing Paul. Even in high school, he had been the standout runner, so having someone internal pushing him was foreign territory. On the fourth repeat, Nigel pulled in a second ahead of Paul at 5:11. The looks on both of their faces acknowledged they were pushing, more like racing rather than training, each with their pride and reputation on the line. Coach had also noticed, but he never cared who won in practice, as long as they hit their times and the splits were negative.

Everyone's attention was glued on the pair, watching in disbelief as Paul and Nigel dropped their times to 5:09 by the time they pulled off the track after their sixth repeat.

"Alright, when you finish, give me ten more minutes as a cool down; then, stretch out together before you leave," Coach said.

The team did a mile loop around the same gravel track before jogging another half to the parking lot. Sarah looked back toward the practice track for some time. The path lay inside a bowl of mountains on three sides. Aside from the coach yelling, it was such a peaceful place. She had missed being out here and, more importantly, she looked forward to the long runs through the rest of the park.

As the stretch circle broke apart, Sarah grabbed two towels from her trunk and placed them on the front seats. It was always nice to have a towel to dry off and sit on for the ride back. Wrapping up her post-workout routine of jogging, stretching, loosening up her shoelaces, and drying off, Sarah looked around and noticed the lot was almost empty. Coach was the only straggler, as he always waited to be sure no one had car trouble before leaving. Sarah looked over to Emily, "I'm all set."

Driving back to campus, they stopped by the dining hall. By this point, the bulk of the team was inside. They had claimed their own secluded section, pulling a few tables together like a family-style meal at a reunion. Since classes had started on a Friday, the celebratory return from summer meal was a school favorite, chicken tenders with mashed potatoes, green beans, freshly baked rolls, and homemade gravy. This main meal was simply missed by anyone who left for the weekend. Since this was the beginning of the semester, the next two weekends would consist of Saturday morning mid-distance runs, and Sunday long recovery runs, leaving no time to return home. Aside from the team, a few students whose parents lived far away, and a group that just never left, the campus was sparse.

Over the course of dinner, the conversation shifted toward the practice earlier that day. Ralph was starting to question Paul on his new rival. "What was going on out there Paul? Is he just being showy, or do you think he is that good?" Sarah could tell Paul was annoyed at being hounded with questions. "Don't worry, he is over on the other side," said Ralph.

"We will see, Ralph. Our first race is in a few weeks, and that's where it matters."

"Yeah true, but there is just one thing, Paul. You could make school history if you were to repeat from last year, but do you think you can make the All-American list with Nigel tripping you up?"

CHAPTER 3:

Black Butterflies

In the heat of August, the presence of black butterflies clouded the trails, hovering around like a ghostly figure wandering the woods. At this point in the season, it was still just weeks of practices, the guys running around one hundred miles and the top girls hitting eighty miles each week. Staying hydrated was key; not enough liquid and overheating or, worse, kidney failure became an ominous reality.

Sarah was on a two-and-a-half-hour run. Nothing crazy, but a decent pace to give her an eighteen-mile-long run for the week. Most of the time, these long runs were accompanied by Emily, or even a few times with Paul, but her and Emm's schedules were off today, so she spent this run left with her thoughts.

Another black butterfly fluttered across the trail in front of her. Trying to occupy her mind, she thought back on earlier in the day when she was sitting outside on the commons.

Minutes might have passed, or even hours. However, time was of no essence. The important thing was what Sarah's eyes and concentration had been focused on.

After spreading a towel out over the grass, Sarah lay out on the green, her close-fitting white denim shorts and baby blue tank-top emphasizing the glow of her cream-toned body. Then, after relaxing in the sun for some time, Sarah momentarily looked up from the book she was reading. It was at that point her eyes caught a butterfly. She noticed the intricate design depicted on the insect's wings. The idea left her deep in thought on how prominently the patterns appeared. What this particular arrangement meant eluded her. Still she wondered, *Why does a butterfly have such designs?* However, this thought only led to a more generic quandary.

All living things seem to display and even follow patterns, she thought. *And so, it seems that just like different butterflies, we define and classify individuals by the patterns they display. Moreover, we classify people by the patterns they follow. In a sense, people are what they do. People are creatures of habit, and habits are no more than patterns that have formed through continuous repetition. Good or bad, we are the things we do, think, believe, and display.*

Really, they make up everything. The conversation from Abstract even stemmed around grouping numbers by different rules, which intern produced a unique arrangement.

As most runners will profess, the mind wanders while out on a long run, covering any topic that aids in distracting from how much time and effort is being put forth.

As her mind drifted from the insect, Sarah turned her focus yet again, this time to the talk of Nigel and Paul competing for the coveted top spot. However, soon her thoughts drifted deeper, pausing briefly on her submerged feelings toward Paul, but eventually she landed on something further back.

Seventeen. That was her age the first time she harbored genuine feelings toward a guy. As the relationship grew, she made a promise. Sarah and her boyfriend Wesley had decided to wait until marriage. Whether from her raising or her own views, even after they split up, the standard stuck. No one else had captured her heart like Wesley had, and their special bond never seemed paralleled. Planning their future together, they would both be happy staying in the same small town, raising a couple of kids, and living a simple life—something back then that felt certain, not based solely on words, but feelings.

The first realization was so intense the longing to tell him and finally pop the cap off the bottled-up emotion scared her. She kept the secret concealed the entire night: the walk in the park, the drive to the theater, and the final moments sitting on the back porch steps.

There was silence as the small talk had faded. The two sat, nuzzled together, gazing into each other's eyes. There were faint noises of the night echoing around them, but neither flinched at such distractions. All their thoughts were centered on that moment and what would happen next. Sarah had questioned if she should say it first, but who knew if he would feel the same. Or even more worrisome, how he would react.

There is something funny about true love. Sometimes, one person realizes it sooner than the other does. The counterpart, the other person is usually just a few steps behind, trying to sort through the butterflies, mixed emotions, and overwhelming thoughts of forever.

Slowly, he leaned in and gave her a kiss on the lips. Then just as cautiously, he moved away. "Sarah, there is something I've been thinking about." She could feel her heart start to fall to her stomach. Before she could respond, he reached over, clasping her hand. "I've lost sleep contemplating how to say this, but I want to tell you…" he paused for a breath. "I love you."

The words hit with such relief that Sarah smiled as she took a deep look into his eyes. "I love you, too."

The world appeared to stop, but time did not. They merely settled into a perfect moment. That moment was magical … but more importantly, pure. Looking back, the simplicity spoke volumes as both were madly in love.

Sarah was not sure how time could slip away so easily. Eventually, the kissing ceased, and they lay in each other's arms, promising to never let go. Just then, her mom would intentionally open the door to let Daisy, their dog, out. Sarah recognized the signal for time to come inside. Once Daisy pawed at the door to be let in, Sarah knew not to press her luck. Reluctantly, they would pull away. Wesley would take her hand and together walk around to the front steps, only to steal one last kiss before going their separate ways for the week. A week of longing and distance that hindered the relationship, only to be fulfilled with the promise of the weekend that lay ahead.

They had met the summer after her sophomore year in high school. Wesley had just graduated and Sarah would be a junior the following year. Although the timing could not have been better, it could have not been so far off. Every day was spent together over the summer: going to the pool, watching the moon, and planning a life together, knowing the arrival of autumn would tear them apart as he left for college. They vowed to not let that stop them. And for months, they didn't.

As Sarah awoke from her daydream, the last glimmers of sunlight faded through the tree leaves. Luckily, she was just in sight of the trailhead. It amazed her how quickly time passed. She was tired, but instead of covering the trail on foot, she felt as though she had just stepped off her own personal transit system, kind of like the moving sidewalks at the airport, but with the ability to climb rocky hills and descend them with greater speed and agility.

As she dried the trails of sweat from her face and arms, Sarah took one look back as the illuminated woods faded to dark. The fiery sky shone with the last of daylight as the sun sunk behind the mountaintops. Now time had come for the diner she coveted.

Following the drive back and a quick shower, Sarah stood in the doorway to Emily's room, waiting for her roommate to finish combing her hair. "You ready?" inquired Sarah.

"Almost."

As Emily gave in to the tussle and reached for her purse on the back of the chair, she heard a big sigh come from Sarah. "Are you okay? Long day?"

Sarah shook her head as to shake off her lethargy. "I just got a little light-headed. I think I just need to get some food in me."

"Tonight is supposed to be chicken parmesan for dinner—my favorite," said Emily. "That will fill you up."

As the two left, Sarah checked her purse to make sure she had her student badge with her. Unsure where she had put the card, she ran her hand along the inside pocket. Behind a tampon, her hand landed on the crisp edges she hoped to find. Pulling the card out, she remembered she was still about a week from starting her period this month. She had always been regular, almost clockwork as she could always predict when Lady Time was about to visit, arriving as expected each month.

After peering up from her bag, Emily walked by and offered to drive, assuming Sarah had misplaced her keys. "Oh, alright!" Sarah murmured. The two shut to the door and hopped into Emily's slightly old, however not yet classic, Oldsmobile.

Only a few parking spots remained in front of the building, forcing Emily to pull into an adjacent lot. Most nights, the team or at least some of them would meet up after a workout to chow down. Between those that were roommates, running buddies, and meal patrons, there was not a day, or even a few hours, that went by without bumping into someone on the team.

Inside, Ralph was standing in the hot line next to the stir-fry. The two girls snuck around in half hopes of startling him. "Excuse me sir, but that's my plate you have there." Without missing a beat, Ralph turned to them, stuck the plate to his face, and licked across the surface.

"Oops, here ya' go. It's all clean now." With a chuckle, he turned back around and handed it to the lady for a heaping of mashed potatoes. Ralph was the comedian of the team. Even on race day, he would try to crack a joke at the starting line. Once the race began, he often struck up conversations with random competitors. It must have been his way to mentally weaken other runners as he showed off his abnormal lung capacity. One year, after the first race, Coach Cavlere had pulled Ralph aside for a stern discussion about how races should be serious, but everyone else knew that was just how Ralph worked.

After going through the line, the three grabbed their drinks and found a table. Over the next hour or possibly two, the trio laughed over the stories from the past year and summer.

"I don't get it," piped Ralph. "What's the big deal if in our off-season I do cross training and coach's workouts, so long as I get faster?"

"What about the new guy, Ralph?" ask Emily.

"Oh, Nigel?" said Ralph.

"Yeah, I'm not too worried about him. You know how newbies are. Got to show off at practice. I think Coach has his doubts about him too. He puts up a good front, but it is all about the race."

All the workouts and long runs left most of the team wanting a little more to eat each night. Maybe that is how it started, or maybe it had always been a tradition of sorts, but as each of them finished the main meal, they wandered over to the cereal aisle. The bar held an assortment of all the imaginable delicious boxes, along with a few healthier picks. Yet, no matter whether the choice was sugary or grainy, white or chocolate milk, cereal was the one thing that topped off each nightly gathering.

Sarah picked up a box of Coco Puffs, poured a bowl about half full, and then reached for the chocolate milk. Chocolate on chocolate, a little guilty pleasure of hers. Not only was her body craving her monthly dose of chocolate, but the idea was run hard enough, and the body would burn anything as fuel.

Bowls in hands, they met back at the table. Ralph had concocted a mix of three cereals, consisting mainly of chocolate and cinnamon. "I made some crazy, crunchy, cookies!" he exclaimed.

"How is that even good? I get the double chocolate part, but mixed with cinnamon?" questioned Emily.

"Keeps your taste buds awake and on the edge," defended Ralph.

Sarah did not think she could describe Ralph better herself as Ralph was always running wide awake and on-edge. Unofficially, this was his mantra to life.

During the season last year, the team had been running a ten-miler at a brisk pace. During the first four miles, Sarah and Emily were hanging with the guys. Along the trail, the forest floor dropped off into a pool of water. Without hesitating, Ralph ran over the edge and leapt off a fifteen-foot waterfall. As he surfaced, he swam to the side of the pool, got out, and continued to run with the group, hardly missing a stride. Of course, the whole time after, his shoes squeaked as the water sloshed around. When they returned to the parking lot, Ralph peeled off his shoes, along with a large blister, proceeding to show everyone the trophy he had been carrying the last six miles.

After dumping their trays, they walked back outside into the still humid August air. Ralph bid Sarah and Emily goodnight before hopping on his bike and flying down the street through the center of campus. "Want to walk around the quad?" suggested Emily.

"Yeah, sure," Sarah replied.

The first few weeks of class were always lively around the school. No tests had been scheduled, assignments had yet to pile up, and finals were a distant thought. A few guys were down on the field throwing a Frisbee around, so the two sat to watch. Sarah soon started gazing up at the sky. She had one more year of college, and she knew it was going to be some of the best times of her life. Sarah longed to soak in that moment: her best friend by her side, a soft chatter from below, the ambient lights that lit up the outline of the campus, and a new season for cross-country. This would be a prime year for them to go to nationals as a team. Paul and Nigel would be leading the guys, and she and Emily, the girls.

CHAPTER 4:

Two-a-Days

When the alarm started buzzing at 5:30 a.m. on Wednesday, it signaled a 6:00 a.m. two-a-day practice. Coming off the long summer months, keeping a distance base was the key to having success throughout the fall. Throwing a two-a-day practice into the mix was the only way to have substantial mileage each week while still producing mile repeats.

As Sarah heard the alarm, she rolled over to hit the off button. Having practice this early was her favorite part about running. With the late August sun still beating down, having a cool brisk breeze to consume a few miles in was somewhat refreshing.

After changing into a pair of three-inch inseams and pulling on a sports bra and shirt, she laced up her shoes before checking on Emily, rapping on the door. "Are you up, Emm?" A slow grumble came from the other side. Sarah cracked opened the door to find Emily still lying in bed. Unable to resist, Sarah ran and jumped on the bed beside her. "Get up, sleepy head. We have practice." Reluctantly, Emily pulled herself from under the covers.

Within just a few seconds, Emily tugged on her running attire and was fumbling with her shoes. "Instead of driving to campus, Emm, do you want to take our bikes?"

"I guess that can be our warmup." Shaking her head laughing, Sarah left the room, with Emily following grudgingly.

The five-mile trek along the road passed by the lake and then up along the ridge of the surrounding hills. Morning runs were conducted in hushed silence. Everyone was still in the process of waking up while trying to control their breathing. Traffic on the roads was sparse in the desolate town. The only noises that broke a conscientious runner's thoughts were the soft chirps of crickets and the pounding of feet along the sidewalks. Even though this run was to be completed at a recovery pace, no one was speaking as the dim shadows trudged alone in unison between streetlamps.

After they rounded the lake and began to climb, Sarah was thinking about the upcoming race. She had already been hitting the desired splits for this point in the season. It was just a matter of putting the race together. With Emily right beside her in practice, the two were looking comfortable as top contenders, as long as no rivals pulled out PRs greater than fifteen seconds. If they continued progressing like last year, a sub 17:20 5K would be in reach by the end of the season.

By the time they crested the top of the hill, the sun had begun to peer over onto the lake. The red glow shone on the water, mirroring fire dancing along the surface. A smooth breeze swept over from the other side. Sarah sighed at the sight and took in a deep breath.

They continued back down the trail to the base, and then back around the lake, up along the road, ending at the school. Overall, Sarah and Emm had maintained about a 7:30 pace, finishing just a few minutes behind Paul and Nigel.

"Good job, everyone; now go hit the showers and head to class. We have a seven-mile run this afternoon, so make sure to rehydrate," said the coach.

Sarah and Emily had about thirty minutes before class started, so instead of sticking around to chat, they left as soon as Coach released them.

Halfway back to their apartment Sarah pulled over, stopping with her bike hinged between her legs. Her eyes had begun to blur, her head started to spin. *That's weird*, she thought.

"Everything alright, Sarah?" Emm called.

"I just got a little dizzy is all," she said as she took her water bottle from the cage and splashed some on her face, and then took a few gulps before peddling off. Even as they parked their bikes, the uneasiness had not subsided. *Maybe I just need a post-run snack.* She went in and grabbed an apple before jumping into the shower. The rush of sugar seemed to help because once she was dressed and headed to class, she felt fine.

For Wednesdays, Sarah had planned her first class for eight o'clock. She was already up from the morning run but still had enough time to get ready. To make matters better, she was taking game theory with Dr. Strom. Dr. Strom was tactful, catching students unprepared by calling on them to keep their attention.

"For today's lecture topic we are covering a highly sought question. How do you fight something that is an instinct? Or, really, the better question is, why would you fight something that is supposed to happen? Biologically, reproduction is what defines your fitness level. The more viable progeny you produce, the greater your fitness level. Then, there's the math standpoint which … well mathematically, it's a little more complicated.

"In our world, we work to predict outcomes. If we know with certainty what the outcome will be, there are no options to weigh and no risks to analyze. In these instances, we make rules and laws to set up the structures that govern such patterns. But, like most things in life, courtships are full of uncertainties.

"Game theory is how we compute the best possible strategy for how to approach these situations. There are four possible choices to court-ing. The female can choose to make the male wait until she feels he will commit to the relationship, or she can allow the male to engage in coitus from the start in hopes he will stick around. The ultimate decision then lies in the hands of the male player. After the courtship is complete, the male can choose to stay with the female, or go off and possibly find another to mate with. If he leaves, the female is left to raise the young alone.

"Now pay attention to the details of how this class will operate. You will be helping me co-teach this semester. What does that mean? I will spend the Monday and Wednesday time frames teaching you new mate-rial. On Fridays, you take turns teaching and explaining a problem from the homework set. This new method of learning will seem a little strange at first given every other lecture you attend is just note- and test-taking. You can only be taught so much from your professors. The idea is that, eventually, you become effective at teaching yourself. That's what we are going to do here.

"You will also be paired into groups. Everyone will be required to give presentations throughout the semester. The more you present, the better your grade can be. There will be other roles as well. Each group will have a leader that oversees who gets to present. During the semester, you will be asked to prepare a special proof, better known as an original research project. This project will consist of a complex proof that will require you to expand on your reasoning in a unique manner.

"Think of the layout as a point system. Then, based on how well each of you do, I can determine your total grade."

Presentations? Sarah thought. Throughout school, she had never been comfortable standing in front of others. The few times she recalled, such humiliation still haunted her. She peered around the room to see if anyone else appeared to share her feelings. Only a few settled back in their chairs, as most seemed intrigued by the idea. Wheeling her head around, she stopped momentarily. Until this point, Sarah had failed to notice Nigel sitting in the back corner. His sight was focused on the board, not entranced in note-taking, but fixed on the professor's plan.

"Oh, and lastly, before class next time, make sure you look over the problem sets on the board. Each has a different setup, and one of them will be on your quiz next week." Checking her watch, Sarah packed her notes into her bag, intent on stopping by the restroom before the next class.

The walk down from science class offered a brief break in Sarah's day. The collection of intermural sports on the green left her longing to join in, but there would be no time today. Walking back into the math building, Sarah descended the stairs to the basement of Boyd. A cool dip in temperature and the hush in the hall made for eerie classrooms. Since the prior semester, Sarah had started working random shifts in the math-tutoring lounge. The job came as a surprise when her calculus professor approached her about the opening. "I could manage working there in between practice and classes," she remembered saying. "And a part-time job would be nice." With Sarah's consideration and a complimentary reference from her professor, she started helping students two weeks later.

The assigned room was tucked away at the far end of the corridor. Few students ventured down to the remote location. Whether they were detoured by a haunted feeling or lack of will to seek tutoring, Sarah was unsure. No matter, the lounge, as it had been called to promote a welcoming vibe, was quiet and tranquil. The regular visitors were a mix of commuters sleeping in the rugged recliners, and a select group of struggling math students.

Easing the door open slightly, Sarah peered in to see whom she would be working with. She enjoyed all the students that reached out for her help, but today had been long and far from over. Quietly, Sarah swung the door the rest of the way open. A few nappers lay sprawled in the dusty yet comfy loungers, but there were no students waiting to greet her. Instead, an auburn-haired girl sat at the corner desk, working diligently. Sarah positioned herself to look over the girl's shoulder. The lack of struggle integrating the equations did not catch her attention. Instead, the realization of knowing the girl steered Sarah to speak up.

"Abby? Right?" A noticeable shudder traversed the toothpick frame of her body, as she turned carefully around.

"Oh! Hi, Sarah! Yeah, I'm Abby."

"Sorry, I didn't mean to catch you off guard," Sarah said.

"That's alright. I was wrapped up in a problem."

"I can help you if you like. At least, that's why I'm here."

"Thank you, but I just came down here to work. This place is so much quieter than the library."

"Sometimes, a little too quiet." Their laughter carried out into the hallway, but the nappers paid no attention.

"How are you feeling about joining the team?" asked Sarah.

"I love it so far. The practices are more rigorous than I anticipated but a challenge I can handle. You and Emily are amazing. Hopefully I can build my way up to your level," replied Abby.

"Ah, thanks, Abby. With Coach's training and that kind of determination, I have no doubts you will," said Sarah. "Speaking of Emily, I know we all have not gotten acquainted with one another yet, but you are welcome to ride out with us to practice. The drive is nice, but it can be creepy if you come back alone in the dark."

"Ha! I know what you mean. I drive most every night back to my room by myself, but luckily, I am adjusting to the idea." Abby continued, "I really appreciate the offer, but I would be an inconvenience."

"Nah. And we can wait on you after class," Sarah offered again, but saw Abby looking timidly up at her instead. And then attempting to ease the subject, she added, "Either way, though."

"Honestly, I just never know where I will be," Abby explained, coaxed by Sarah's puzzled expression. "I work at a restaurant just outside town, usually at night, or if I have a few hours throughout the day that I can spare from studying or running."

A smile came over Sarah's face, half relieved that Abby was not avoiding her but instead opening up.

"That makes sense. I was beginning to think you'd rather not be around us," Sarah joked.

"Not at all. Right now, I just save what I can, and hopefully will have an easier semester in the spring," Abby replied.

"I hope so. Then you can join us for dinner and maybe lunch," Sarah said.

"I would like that. Well, I do need to finish up before practice, but thanks for offering."

"Anytime, Abby. I will see you at the park," Sarah said, and took a seat at the desk in the center of the room while Abby continued scribbling in the corner. She waited, but no students walked in through the door. But the semester had barely started, so the emptiness would end.

When her shift finally came to an end, Sarah headed to meet Emily. Because of their early-morning run, Coach had advised everyone to meet at a small park about a mile from campus. They would only be completing a sixty-minute run, no racing or fast tempo. A settling assignment. Since Tuesdays were built around speed and endurance, Wednesdays were for a leisurely run, or as close as Coach would allow. Moreover, since Emily had scheduled her labs for Wednesday nights, Sarah knew she would have a few hours to herself, a time she would center not just on studying but also on relaxing.

Running around the outer perimeter of the parking lot and edges of the tree line, the hour was passed conversing and running circle after circle in the loop. "Hey Emm, are you biking to your lab tonight, or driving?" Sarah asked as she looked at the lingering gray clouds in the distance.

Emily, noticing her stare, said, "I guess I will be driving now."

"Okay, I just wanted to see if I needed to pick you up."

"I will be fine; just need to make sure I get there in time to park close to the building."

When they came around, passing the drop point for a third time, the outskirt of a storm was beginning to consume the sky. The two checked their watches, calling time at sixty-three minutes. Coach had joined in for the run, and they could see him making his way around from the far side of the park. The team was beginning to gather, but following a loud pop of lightning, the group stretch switched to a shortened version.

"Take it to the house!" yelled Coach as he cut through a field to pick up two of the freshmen.

Hastily, Sarah and Emily followed his command, leaving promptly for their apartment. Even with the extra time on hand, Emily went to her class without showering, still wearing her running clothes. Not really permissible for lab, but Emm was determined to not walk in the rain.

As Sarah nestled on her bed, book in lap, she stared out the open window. The leaves of the maple tree shuddered yet held tight to the branches as the breeze breached the windowpane, warning of the forth-coming storm.

Sarah was reminded of her studying as she found her glasses slipping down the bridge of her nose. However interesting biology normally was, she could not find the motivation to concentrate. Her attention was again interrupted as she reached for a blanket. Folded at the post of her bed lay a patchwork quilt her grandmother had fabricated to remind her of where she came from. This had lodged in her heart ever since. The diverse pieces, each with their own individual meaning, represented a part of a whole. Much like the leaves on a tree, one leaf does not complete the picture, but when sewn together, a vibrant whole is formed. It was amazing how something so simple could mean so much. Nothing elegant or showy, but quaint.

Not until after summoning the mindset to finish the study session did Sarah remove her blanket, and get up from her bed. Walking over to the bathroom, Sarah turned on the faucet for the hot water and undressed, placing a bathrobe around her bare skin.

The dripping of the faucet was the only disruption. Sarah cut the tap off as the bubbles finally rose to the rim of the tub. She unfastened her robe and hung it on the rack. She slid her foot into the steaming water before stepping into the haven of bubbles and immersing her body in the froth of foam. The film buried her body up to her chest. As she sank lower, she let out a soft gasp.

The weekly bubble bath was her refuge from all the training and class work. The thoughts and troubles that usually clouded her mind were swept away by this familiar utopia. She was not sure why a simple bubble bath gave her such comfort. Maybe it was her way of reverting to childhood, but just having a nurturing environment of warm water, foaming suds, and scented soaps gave her a sense of serenity.

Sarah picked up the razor placed on the side of the tub, running the metal effortlessly along the contours of her leg toward the apex of her knee. Jettisoning all the fine hairs revealed a silky canvas of skin. Bubbles rose and fell on her chest with each shallow breath taken in the tranquil pool. Scents of sweet pea and clover draped the air of the room. All that remained was basking in the effervescence of her steaming bubble bath.

The paradise reminded her of the desire to indulge in the simple innocent pleasures found in life. The cover of bubbles fortified a harbor that fostered the childish tendencies that flourished within her soul. Scalding water thrust her body into a subtle state of shock that exiled all fears, disappointments, and figments of stress. The tightness that engulfed the deepest of muscles released upon sinking further into the tub.

When the water became tepid, Sarah began to drain the bath, washing off the suds as the water level dropped. Soon her bared chest, chilled from the air, drew notice to her nakedness. Stepping out of the tub, she wrapped the robe around her and tied the sash.

Sarah debated whether to put on a pair of jeans or just slip into her pajamas. The thought of curling up in a pair of sweats, pulling a carton of ice cream out of the freezer, and watching a romance on television seemed most desirable. However, Sarah decided to pull out a cute shirt with a pair of her favorite jeans. There was something satisfying about dressing up for just herself. The gratification was like finding an old charm that, once polished, had a new glow about it.

Now sitting on the bed with a box of chocolate chip cookies and a pedicure kit, she rummaged through the bag looking for a certain color nail polish. Stuffed in the corner pocket rested a crumbled piece of paper. Curious, she pulled out the wrinkled parchment. She delicately unfolded the creases, careful not to tear it. When she pulled back the last layer, a smile slipped across her face. It was an old fortune cookie she received years ago, which she had tucked away. *You will only find what makes you happy when you find yourself alone and content.* At the time, she had thought it was just a cute quote that had a Zen vibe. Now as she sat alone, she realized what the message really meant.

Reaching back into the bag, she pulled out the polish she had originally been searching for. After filing down the creases in her toenails, she shook the bottle and began brushing on the lacquer. Sarah never used store-bought spacers or toilet paper to keep her toes from touching. She had always done her own nails, and was methodical in how gingerly she stroked the brush.

With a sigh, she started to sing, soft at first, her voice soothing, almost angelic. She sang just enough to break the quiet of the room, brushing her nails back and forth, ever so carefully to keep the paint from running.

As she finished detailing her little toe, Sarah dipped the brush back into the bottle and tightened the cap. Giving a soft blow over her nails, she was pleased with the dark blue shade cascading along the mini canvases like tiny glacier lakes.

A noise from outside broke her concentration and she looked up at the door. Some of the girls from down the way were either leaving for the night or coming back in. She looked around the room then out toward the window. The storm had covered the city and was now pelting the ground with rain.

Abruptly, her bedroom door sprung open in unison with the crashing of lightning. Emily ran and jumped on the bed beside Sarah as the two cowered together from the startling thunder. Unhooking their clasped hands, they began to laugh at the moment of vulnerability.

"What are you doing back?" Sarah inquired.

"I have to let one of my tests run for thirty minutes then check the results. Everyone left, so I thought I would come back and relax here for a little bit." Emm looked down at Sarah's toes. "I love that color. Do you mind if I do mine?"

"Sure, Emm. I can do your fingernails for you if you want," Sarah replied.

Twisting the bottle open, she examined Emily's nails. She knew she did not have time to file them down, but Emily always kept up on that part of her appearance. Another strike of lightning jolted them as the lights flickered in response. This time, they merely laughed as Sarah smeared the polish off to the slide of Emily's finger. "Just leave it," Emily said, laughing.

"No, no; I want my work to shine," Sarah insisted.

Within a few minutes, she had finished all of Emily's nails. Not bothering to let them dry adequately, only blowing on the fresh polish, Emily bolstered herself up from the bed. "Thanks, Sar. I've got to head back for about another hour, but I will not be too late." Sarah smiled as Emily ran out the door, not lingering long enough for a reply.

Sarah leaned over to the nightstand and picked up the book she had been reading. Alongside the bible lay her reading glasses. Placing them on her nose, Sarah propped the spine open between her legs, leaving the makeshift bookmark tucked in place. Over the past few years, she had grown more accustomed to reading her bible. A few nights each week, she would pick up where she left off or thumb through in search of something meaningful. Tonight, she decided to wander again from the continued reading. As she thumbed through the scritta paper, she landed in Ecclesiastes, Chapter 9, Verse 11: "I returned, and saw under the sun, that the race is not to the swift, nor the battle to the strong, neither yet bread to the wise, nor yet riches to men of understanding, nor yet favour to men of skill; but time and chance happeneth to them all." Sarah adjusted the glasses that sat on the bridge of her nose.

What did this mean? Closing her eyes, she started to pray, searching for better understanding.

When she came to herself, she was not sure how much time had passed. She opened her eyes again, this time trying to clear her thoughts of everything but this single text.

The lids of her eyes hung heavier and lower, until she drifted off asleep, book in her lap, head tilted down, leaning against the wall. She woke just long enough to remove her clothes, retreat under the covers, and place her glasses and bible on the nightstand.

It was three in the morning when a damp cool sensation filled her body, mind, and self. Sarah awoke in a pool of sweat, spanning from the pillow that cradled her head to the sheets that draped over her body. She leapt up frantically. *Did I wet the bed?* she first thought. Pulling a towel from her closet, Sarah positioned the cloth over the sheets, attempting to dry up the moisture. Satisfied with the makeshift blanket, she shimmied back into her bed and placed the slightly damp sheet back over her. With a new feeling of warmth, she dozed off to sleep.

In the morning, Sarah ran her hands once again over the bed sheets. There were no indications that the night before had left her bathed in sweat. Everything was dry. *Was I dreaming?* Even her hair had been soaked, but now as she patted her head, she noticed if anything the texture seemed oily. She leaned over to smell her pillow. Unlike running socks or gym clothes laced with sweat, there was no lingering scent of briny body odor. She shook her head in confusion. *Maybe I was just sleep walking, got cold, and grabbed a towel.* Nonetheless, she pulled the covers from the bed and tossed the sheets into the hamper, pulling a fresh set from the closet and remade her bed.

CHAPTER 5:

Racing

B eval's empty streets flurried each semester after a barren summer. Thursdays during the late summer nights called for all students to venture outside of campus. Each for a different purpose would ready for a night on the town.

Sarah arrived at Bruno's wearing her favorite blue jean shorts with an orange top. Her hair lay typically straight along her shoulders and down her back, held flawless on the breezy evening. She was arm-in-arm with Emily as they entered the restaurant.

Bruno's was their usual going-out place. It was everyone's usual place. The city was a small town that only played host to two main venues, Bruno's and a cliquey place called Rafter. As the two girls pranced through the doors, they landed at the high-top table at the far corner of the room.

"Hello, ladies. Will y'all be having the usual?" said the waiter, as the girls settled in on their chairs.

"Hi, Jason. Yes, please."

"Sure thing; I'll get that right out."

The music was a soothing, welcoming trance of beats that took the edge off a loaded week. Sarah always became easily lost in the euphoria created by the atmosphere much like someone sequesters their mind into a free state while filling their blood with adrenaline.

"You know what?" said Sarah. "I love being back in this town, but school is going to be much tougher this year with all upper-level classes, and coach is going to be pushing us for regional titles."

Emily gave a slight smirk. "Isn't that what college is all about? Think about it, if we could just train all the time, without school and home-work, what would we do in our free time?"

"Ha! Maybe read a book or catch a movie," replied Sarah.

"Right, but part of pushing yourself to be the best anything is know-ing you can balance everything else in life," Emily continued.

"Yeah, you are right, Emm, but who knows what we could do if that was our sole focus."

"Try to focus on this, Sarah. Here come our plates."

"Here you are girls. Anything else I can get for you?"

"Maybe some chips and your homemade guacamole?"

"Coming right up!" said Jason.

As Sarah sat there picking away at her meal, she remembered when she first came to Bruno's at the end of her first spring semester. It was after their exams in May, and there were a few weeks where the team had to stick around and train preemptively for nationals. Only two members were competing, but coach wanted everyone to get used to training longer. At that point in the year, everyone had left campus, and there was nowhere to go in town except Bruno's.

Looking across the way, Sarah noticed Nigel walk in with a few guys she did not recognize. "Who do you suppose they are?" she questioned.

Carelessly, Emily replied, "Dunno; probably just some of his roommates. You aren't going to invite him over, are you?" She didn't have to think long on the proposition, as she quickly turned her head.

"He looks occupied with his friends. I just never see him with anyone from the team. Maybe if he was alone, but I'd rather have a girl's night."

As the two continued eating, Nigel stayed over to the side with his group. Sarah doubted they had even caught his eye. With one last swoop of her chip into the bowl, she looked down at her watch. "Are you ready?" Emily nodded in agreement, as she had a mouthful of chips and salsa. The two slid out of their seats, grabbing their purses as they headed toward the door. Sarah took a final glance in Nigel's direction before walking out. He must have taken notice of her gesture, for when she looked around he was smiling back toward her. Sarah dimly smiled but only lingered for a second before following Emily outside.

The short walk home ended with Sarah bidding Emily goodnight. Emm veered off to the kitchen for dessert as Sarah headed up the stairs. With each step, the excitement of the night faded to anxiousness. Now, only one day stood between her and the first race of the season.

The opening race always drummed up mixed emotions. Unsettling nerves and jitters began to creep back into consciousness after being at bay for months of not racing. Yet, this fear was accompanied by the readiness to see the long summer of high mileage pay off.

Sarah and Emily had the same prerace routine. Starting with a big serving of pasta, they covered the noodles with goat cheese, ground pepper, and creamy Prego with mushrooms thrown into the mix. Over dinner, they discussed how they hoped the race would unfold, casting aside any doubts with reassurance. To top off the carb loading, Emily concocted smoothies made of frozen strawberries, bananas, and milk, each cup blended until the chunks of ice meshed into froth. Sarah sipped from her cup while flipping through a *Runner's Junky* magazine, as Emily iced her legs.

Although Emily struggled with early mornings, she had no plans of going to bed early. There was nothing left to do but to pack their bags, yet Emily would not fall asleep until after eleven or maybe twelve. The night before a race never held promises of sleep for any runner, but Sarah always tried to settle down around nine.

The well-broken-in duffle bag was shoved under her bed following each race. She bent over grudgingly as the bulk of her food pushed out her bloated stomach. Unable to locate the strap by feel, Sarah laid down on her stomach, sticking her head under the dust ruffles. The duffle lay hidden behind a smudged pillow and fleece blanket bundled together. She stretched out over the floor. Barely reaching the closest strap, Sarah pulled, dragging all three. Both the pillow and blanket had been washed following track, but the lingering bus smell remained. Tucked in the bottom of the bag lay her spikes for track and cross-country. Placing the tar battered shoes back underneath, she rose up. Neatly folding the blanket and stuffing the pillow inside the bag, she zipped up the spikes on the side. The bag closed, Sarah placed her warmups and uniform on top, readied for the morning.

Winding down was almost as methodical, but did not always deliver the desired rest. A ten-minute steaming shower was enough time to relax her muscles and give her legs a shave. Five o'clock would come early in the morning.

The morning of a race, Sarah always skipped breakfast. There was just one problem. On early mornings like this, she always felt sick. Not having eaten since dinner often made her nauseous, and attempting breakfast made her vomit. For years, she did not know how to handle the situation. She had to find a way to calm her stomach or possibly jeopardize the race. In high school, her mom had suggested some fizzy water or a soft drink as an alternative. She settled on trying to drink a small glass of pop. After a few sips, her stomach issues would subside with no further problems.

Walking out of the kitchen, Sarah bent over to pick up her bag. She ran her hand up the front, then down the back of her calf, checking to make sure the shave the night before would suffice for the day. She noticed the light upstairs shut off. A bleary-eyed Emily rounded the corner, saying, "I'm ready, almost forgot to get my spikes."

When they pulled into the school parking lot, the bus was already sitting idle and loaded with the team. Sarah always got to the bus just a few minutes before 5:30 am, leaving time to spare. Today, however, as they loaded the bus, only three seats remained open after others had loaded the drinks and snacks or sprawled out asleep. One opening was beside Coach, another by Ralph and the last next to Nigel. "I call the seat with Ralph," whispered Emily.

Sarah decided to sit with Nigel since he was the lone ranger with whom no one else wanted to share a seat. She unrolled the blanket and took the pillow out of her bag before plopping down beside him. "Hope you don't mind," she said.

"All is well," Nigel replied.

"I am not much for the long morning rides," stammered Sarah. "They always crank up the cold air, like they want to keep us awake for the whole trip."

"Oh, I love a little air conditioning blaring while I am kicking back taking a nap."

The bus doors were starting to shut when Paul came sprinting up the stairs. "Sorry I'm late; overslept!" he bellowed. Everyone grumbled at the disturbance. Paul peered over the rows of heads to find an empty seat. His eyes stopped for a second when he saw Sarah and Nigel, before he settled for the open seat next to Coach.

For the most part, Sarah tried to go back to sleep on the bus. The half-reclining chairs were not always the most comfortable, nor did they provide the best positioning for sleeping. However, Sarah hunkered down in the chair and pulled her blanket up tight.

"Are you excited for the race?" Nigel asked Sarah.

Sarah had not spent much time talking to Nigel, and she did not really want to strike up a conversation this early in the morning. However, her compassion got the best of her.

"Ah, a little nervous. I always get that way until the race starts, especially since we haven't raced recently. How about you?" she replied.

"Old Paul and I are going to go out strong together for the first three miles, then after that it is every man for himself."

"That's a good plan. Me and Emm usually end up together throughout most the race, or at least fairly close."

"Yeah, always helps to have a little competition to get you in gear. You sure were smart to bring a blanket, they must think it's supposed to be the subarctic in here," he chattered as the temperature fell now that the doors were closed. Nigel had just worn his shorts and T-shirt, no sweats or even a long tee.

"Yeah, zero or one hundred degrees are the only settings, but still better than being stuffy and hot; then no one can sleep. This blanket is pretty big if you want to share. No use in you freezing the whole way."

"Oh wow! That would be great," Nigel said. Then, he lifted the covers and pulled in closer to Sarah. Thankfully, the chair arm served as a divider, keeping them each in their own space. Sarah plumped her pillow to get the firmness just right, and then drifted off back to sleep.

When they arrived at the course, Sarah jumped slightly at the abrupt sound of the bus releasing air pressure. The sun had hardly risen, casting hues of pinks and oranges along the cloudy sky.

"Alright, let's go!" commanded Coach. "Guys, in this race, you are up in forty-five minutes, and then the girls start right after their finish."

The rush of excitement subsided as the guys finished their stretches on the line. A lanky official made his way to the center of the field, causing a calmness about the air. With the sound of the gun, Paul and Nigel took off in the lead pack. As the group hurtled down the open field and toward a turn, the two were boxed in, causing Paul to double step a few times and Nigel to almost fall. Luckily, when they emerged around the bend, only one guy had tripped and was now bringing up the rear.

As they circled around for their first mile, the rusty colored skies transformed to a translucent gray, spotted with darker patches of clouds. From just a few drops, a sprinkle forced its way into a drizzle, the drizzle paced itself into a steady rain, and by the time the guys were coming through mile four, the skies had opened, allowing the rain to consume the course.

Sarah and Emily had been cheering for them at each mile marker. Nigel was just ahead of Paul, with Ralph about ten seconds back with the rest of the team.

Sarah knew they could not sit still long, or their body temperatures would begin to cool down. Unwillingly pulling away from the action, Sarah and Emily decided to head back toward the tent to switch into their running spikes.

As the tent came into view, the girls could see and feel Coach's fury as he yelled instructions. "Let's go, ladies. Girls already had their first and second call. The director wants to get these races completed before the thunderstorms come in."

Sarah plopped down on the tarp to change her shoes. The cold water that soaked into her shorts and up her inner thigh directed her attention to a river of water that had run over from the side. Emily, holding back a laugh in fear of Coach, took note and swapped out her shoes while bracing against a pole. Without missing a beat, they finished transitioning together and ran off to the start line. Their late arrival, followed by the huddle for the prerace team prayer, left only seconds before the crack of the gun.

The intensity of the rain made seeing difficult. Long stretches saturated with water, simulated conditions of trudging through a swamp. Constant pattering of soaked shoes set the tone for blistering toes. Heavy breathing added injury to the mental drainage of the race. About a mile and a half in, the monsoon became a substantial hindrance. Reading the numbers when Sarah looked at her watch was impossible. Whatever the time was, she supposed it was slow. Given her current struggle, doubt crept into her mind. The guys had run just prior to them, leaving the integrity of the course washed away into a slush of mud. Every step was either an effort not to slip or a fight to lift her feet back up from the ankle-deep puddles. Any sloshing sounds from the saturated shoes were now trumped by the pounding of the rain. Yet somehow, Sarah kept running.

"You all call that an effort? I have never seen anything so pathetic in my entire running career!" Instead of doing the preached upon post-race two-mile cool down, the coach ordered everyone to load the bus. Filing silently to their seats, Sarah could hear him murmuring under his breath. No one dared to say a word as he climbed up the stairs, continuing his lecture. For the next ten minutes, he belabored their failure to sprint off the line at the sound of the gun, not using the energy reserves in the first twenty to thirty seconds of the race.

Once he took his seat at the front, Sarah looked over to Emily. They both had gone off the line like any previous time. The only difference was they had gotten boxed in after the first hundred yards in the bottle-neck curve. Coach had warned about this section, but sprinting off the start line? That seemed suicidal. It was not though because for the next two weeks, every practice ended with striding out for twenty seconds at near-race pace with a forty-second break before repeating.

The ride home was quiet. Only the faint noise of music leaking out of earphones broke the silence. Sarah and Emily shared a row that freed up after the post-race snacks were inhaled.

For whatever reason, Emily could sleep anywhere. As a matter of fact, she often tossed her pillow in the middle of the aisle and curled up with her blanket on the floor, but this time, she had stayed nestled in the adjoining seat and was fast asleep. To her dismay, however, Sarah could not get settled. She nudged Emily in hopes that she could accidently wake her up and maybe have someone to talk to. But every effort to disturb her slumber was a lost effort. Finally, she leaned over on the backrest and tilted her head up toward the ceiling. As she sat gazing at the roof, a familiar face obstructed her view.

His uncanny smile broke the awkward silence. Paul was leaning over the seat looking at her as if she had stolen the last of the cookies, but with a willing to share attitude. Sarah cracked a laugh. "Can I help you?" she asked.

"Ha! Oh, it's okay! I was just seeing who was leaning back on me," he said.

"Oh, sorry! I can pull up my chair," Sarah replied.

"No, it is alright, only for you though," he joked.

Sarah smiled, "Why do you think Coach was so grumpy today? The top guys and girls did well considering the conditions."

"You know Coach; he is all about setting impressions, weeding out the new kids, and making sure we are all working," said Paul.

"Yeah, it would probably seem a little out of character for him to be praising our efforts at the beginning of the season," Sarah agreed.

"How are you and Nigel doing?" Sarah asked with a laugh.

"We are fine, just not seat buddies like you and Emm, but we keep a team relationship. I just want to make sure I stay in front of him," he said. Then looking at Emily, he asked, "Is Emily really asleep? I thought she always slept in the floor."

"I guess she changed her mind, because I nudged her a few times and she didn't wake up."

"Are you two headed down to the beach right after we get back?"

"Yeah, that's the plan. From the looks of it, I will be driving down there. Emily will probably go back to sleep in the car."

"Did y'all get a room in the same hotel as ours?"

"No, Emily's aunt has a small, one-bedroom beach house nearby. Her family has a wedding this weekend and said we could use it."

"Ah man! I am rooming with Ralph, but I think all the other guys are staying at the same hotel as us."

"Ours is not right on the beach; it's a short walk across the street."

"Coach overheard the guys talking about the trip last week, and he made it clear that we better get our runs in, otherwise he would make this a mandatory closed weekend."

"Yeah, after you let that slip, he told us the same, and that we better stay in different rooms than the guys."

"You got to love Coach; he is like your parent in some ways, wanting what's best, yet you are more apt to listen."

"I am going to try and get some rest so I can drive when we get back," Sarah said.

Paul looked over at Ralph who was fast asleep. "Not me; Ralph is taking the wheel."

Sarah leaned up to grab her purse from her bag. Retrieving her sunglasses, she tucked the purse to her side opposite of Emily, leaned back, and drifted off to sleep.

CHAPTER 6:

Sandy Clothes

The first weekend in September: the hills of Beval become quiet. Droves of students load their cars with suitcases carrying the last of their summer attire in an escape to the beach. In the midst of cross-country, the three-day weekend was the last opportunity for vacation until November. While some headed home a final time before Thanksgiving and others, like Abby, decided to work an extra shift, Sarah and Emily had set their sights on the ocean.

"Wake up, sleepy head. We're back," said Sarah, but Emily squirmed refusing to open her eyes or budge from the seat. "Don't worry, I will drive down there, but we have to go back to shower and load the luggage."

Convincing Emily to comply, Sarah packed their duffle bags in the trunk of her car.

"Ok, given me fifteen minutes and I will be ready to go," said Sarah.

"Are you not going to shower?" Emily asked.

"Yeah, I need five to shower and ten to change. You know, just wash off the grime and put on comfy clothes for the drive."

"Yeah, but how long does it take you to pack?" questioned Emily.

"I already packed," she laughed. Looking around at Emily, a mischievous expression mixed with a plea for forgiveness caught her eye. "Oh Emm, you haven't packed yet? It's okay; you are pretty fast, so go ahead and take a shower, then pack while I am getting ready. I will go ahead and bring out the snacks and towels and whatever else we need."

Despite their efforts, another hour had passed before the two settled back into Sarah's car. Although, it was a few hours away, the beach was a straight shot down the interstate. Fortunately, Sarah's restless nap on the bus was enough, as she took the wheel for the entire trip.

When the two pulled onto the road alongside the shore, they could see the crowd of the guys' team unpacking in the parking lot. "I bet if we hurry, we can beat them down to the beach. They will never know we fell behind," Emily laughed.

"That would be funny. How about we just unpack the important things. If you put the food in the refrigerator, I'll go park by the pier and pick out a spot on the sand. That way, they will think we have been here a while."

"Sounds good, Sar."

As Emily was putting the last of the groceries up, Sarah dropped her beach bag just above the grasp of the tide. She sat alone on the beach, towel laid over the sizzling surface, toes curled up under the sand. The dark-rimmed glasses with large oval lenses she wore covered the better half of her face. She hunched back on the hands with her legs stretched out from the striped bikini bottoms. The only sound was the crashing waves along the shore. Emily would be on her way down from the house, but until she arrived, Sarah had a few minutes to herself.

The sound echoed in her head. 17:57, 17:58, 17:59 Jessica... 18:00, 18:01 18:02, 18:03 Sarah.... She had been barely out-kicked or merely outrun for first place, followed by Emily about ten seconds back. What a way to start a Labor Day weekend. An intense, close finish made for a good start to the season after a summer of logging more than eight hundred miles. Paul and Nigel also had a close race. They went out in 5:20, finishing at 27:09, Paul beating Nigel by four seconds.

Sarah's thoughts were interrupted when Emily came up beside her. "I saw the guys coming so I ran down here," she laughed. Emily hastily shed her shorts and top, revealing her petite figure. She was only a little shorter than Sarah, yet very small. Despite her tiny frame, her breasts were the same size as Sarah's, meaning they could still borrow each other's shirts and dresses. More importantly, they had the same size feet, so once they became roommates, their choices in shoes doubled.

Emily draped her long, dirty blond hair behind her shoulders as she sat down on the blanket Sarah laid out for her. Placing a cap on her head, Emily leaned back on her hands, her arms straight and her legs bent just enough that she could place the soles of her feet flat.

The sun radiated down upon the sand, heating the specks like small coals from a fire. The mirages created by the waves of heat in front of them formed the image of a desert in the abyss, only succumbing to the crashing waves that splashed a spray of mist from the ocean.

As the guys from the team made their way down off the pier over the dunes, their roasting skin glowed. Although the scalding weather persisted, the heat was welcome. The sun was revitalizing after spending much of the morning soaked during the race.

"Well you girls did make it," berated Paul.

"We beat you though, didn't we?" chimed Emily. Sarah looked over to as the guys joined them. Nigel was carrying two poles wound together in a net, while Ralph was spinning a green ball on the tip of his finger.

"We figured we would set up a game of volleyball. You girls want to play?"

"Only if you want to get beat by a girl," said Emily as she stood up from her towel. "What do you say, Sarah?"

"I think I am just going to watch."

"It's okay, Emily, Sarah is not as tough as you," piped Nigel. With a slight glare, Sarah pulled her knees to her chest, hopping to her feet.

"Only if we could play girls versus guys."

Ralph stopped spinning the ball as his attention was reeled in, and he yelled, "I'll be the ref!"

Ralph and Nigel set up the net while Paul marked off the boundaries. As they finished, Ralph stood back proudly and announced the rules.

"House rules. Each side can hit the ball three times after the ball passes over the net. At that point, if the ball doesn't make it back to the other side, a point goes to the other team. If the ball lands on the boundary marker, it is out of bounds and point to the other team. The first team to eleven wins and the other team has to strip." A big smile covered his face as he announced the final remark.

Without missing a second, Emily turned and assured him, that would only happen in his dreams. "Okay, okay. To decide who gets the ball first, let's play nose goes." At that signal, Sarah and Emily both placed their fingers to their noses in unison.

Nigel and Paul just looked at each other. "Ralph, what are you talking about?"

"No matter, men, the ladies got to their noses first, so they get the ball. Now, for the fun part. What shall the wagers be?"

Both sides stumbled for a moment. A bet could be tricky. If the guys came up with a ridiculous offer, the girls did not want to be undersold, but if they proposed the ridiculous idea themselves, the guys would surely try to come up with something even more outrageous. After some discussion, Paul and Nigel broke from their huddle.

Emily glanced over and then back at Sarah. "I got this," she said.

"Okay, guys, what happens if you win?"

"Ralph, if we win, the girls have to go streaking down the beach tonight."

"Interesting... And, ladies, do you accept?" Before Sarah could refute the offer, Emily jumped in.

"Absolutely, but when we win, the guys agree to wax." Nigel and Paul scoffed at this proposal.

"Wax what, Emm?" asked Nigel.

"Everything," Emily replied.

With a little hesitation, Nigel replied, "You're on!"

"Ladies and gents, we have the deal. Now for the official handshakes."

Emily was the first to shake with Paul and Nigel, but Sarah was still uncertain. She knew she and Emily could probably hold their own, but she was not comfortable with the thought of streaking down the beach. Emily leaned over to elbow her.

"Come on, we got this." Sarah took a deep break and closed her eyes, extended her hand and shook on the deal.

In just a few sets, the guys captured a slight lead. Still, the girls refused to back down, giving them a run for the win. Emily served the role of digger while Sarah played as the hitter. Nigel and Paul struggled with the low balls but sent a few over the girls' heads. As the game continued, the score advanced to a ten–ten tie.

"Game point! Men, you have possession of the ball," said Ralph.

Nigel served from the corner of the court, line driving the ball to Sarah, who was dusting the sand from her bottom. The failure to previously retrieve a ball that soared over her head had left her tumbling backward. Unaware the game had resumed, she looked up just in time to see the ball spiraling toward her, smashing into her face before dropping to the sand.

"We won!" yelled Nigel. Sarah found herself again on the sand. The force left her dazed and unable to see Emily coming over to her side.

"Sarah, can you hear me?" she said. Then shaking her head, Emily returned to address Ralph and Nigel who were high-fiving at this point.

"That doesn't count," said Emily.

"Unfortunately, it does," defended Ralph.

"I called game point and handed off the ball, which means the play is live."

"Well, the deal is off, Nigel."

Paul stooped down to check on Sarah. With a slight wiggle to her noise, he said, "I don't think it's broke or anything; just knocked you for a loop."

Emily and Nigel were now in a heated debate over who won.

"People, people," Ralph scorned. "What if we call it a tie, and both the guys and the girls have to go streaking?"

Nigel refused, but Paul pulled away from evaluating Sarah to agree with the bargain.

"So, it's settled," declared Ralph. "We will meet back here at midnight."

Emily helped Sarah stand and gather their towels. The two girls trekked back across the sand to their car, leaving the guys to converse amongst themselves.

"Emm, I cannot do that; it is too embarrassing."

"Sarah, take it easy. It's going to be dark; no one will be able to see you."

"Still; it's just awkward."

"It will be fine. Just don't run ahead of anyone, and they will hardly notice," she suggested.

The rush of cool air as they opened the front door eased Sarah's throbbing head. She headed into the bathroom and changed out of her swimming suit. As she unclasped her top and slid the right strap down, she could tell she had gotten sunburned. She turned to her bag and found a bottle of aloe. Removing the other strap of her top, she used her left hand to hold the cups against her breasts and her right to apply the aloe where she could reach, before switching hands to reach the rest of her back. When she finished, Sarah continued to hold the suit to her chest and walked out to her bed. Emily had already changed and was eating a snack, so Sarah laid face down on the bed to prevent the ointment from rubbing off on the sheets.

She could hear a knock on the cottage door, but when Emily's voice answered, Sarah strained to hear whom she was speaking with.

"I think she is alright. Let me check." Sarah faked being asleep as Emily cracked the door open to the bedroom. As the knob clicked shut behind her, Sarah got up from the bed. She tiptoed over to the door, trying to overhear the conversation. As she rested her ear upon the door, Sarah barely caught Emily saying, "Don't go in there…" Sarah jutted backward, but it was too late. The knob turned and the door flung open a second later, only giving her time to wrap her arms around her uncovered chest, she was left standing in the middle of the room, exposed.

Paul's eyes landed on Sarah's bare skin, too shocked to avert them. Time stood still as the two looked at each other in silence, only to be broken as Emily filed into the room.

"Get out, Paul," yelled Emily.

"I am so sorry, Sarah. I just wanted to see if you were okay." Emily jumped on his back as she saw Sarah, trying to force his eyes away from her.

"It's alright, Emily. I am going," said Paul, as he continued to apologize. Still standing with Emily on his back and her hands covering his eyes, he turned toward the door briefly before again spinning back around to address Sarah.

"Oh, and don't worry about the bet; I will take care of Nigel." As he made his way blindly to the door, Sarah grabbed her top from the bed, and latched the clips back together.

"Wait." Seeing that Sarah was now dressed, Emily climbed off Paul's back. "A bet is a bet. We will come tonight."

"Are you sure, Sar? I don't mind…," offered Paul.

"Thank you; but I am sure, Paul."

He gave a striking smile as he stepped back to leave. "Alright then."

A pale moon hung high in the sky as they all followed the ambient light to the beach. The few ocean dwellers from earlier had retired for the night and the beach was deserted.

"Emily, there is still enough light from the moon to see if we take off our clothes," Sarah hissed. Emily paid no attention, leaving her to only find solace in seeing no late night strollers to spectate.

Ralph waited excitedly on the shore. "Okay, here is the deal. I have placed two black socks and two white shocks on sticks about fifty meters away. You must strip down, leave your clothes here, run out, and each of you must retrieve a sock. Girls will get the white socks and guys, the black ones. You will get your clothes only in exchange for the correct sock. If you fail to do so or refuse to participate, your clothes will be subject to a stink bomb. Okay, everyone, get naked. I will count down from three."

Nigel and Paul removed their clothes and threw them to the side of Ralph's feet. Emily followed without much delay. Sarah was the last. She closed her eyes before removing her shirt and shorts. Then she unhooked her bra and tossed it to the side. With a surge of disbelief, she pulled her panties to her ankles and kicked them to Ralph. One arm lay over her chest while a hand covered her front.

"Three, two, one, go!" The four sprinted off to the sound of Ralph's voice. They raced down the sandy course, staying within a stride of each other.

Ahead, Emily spotted the sticks. "There!"

As they reached the turning point, Nigel and Emily snatched their respective socks. Sarah, a split second behind, was beat out by Paul taking his and hers. As he turned to run off, he stopped.

"I'm only kidding, Sar," he said tossing the white one back to her. She reached out catching the sock, forgetting the cover of her arms.

Racing back to a now naked Ralph, Emily and Nigel reached their clothes first and were half-dressed by the time Paul and Sarah returned. Handing their socks to Ralph, Paul and Sarah proceeded to put their clothes on.

"Well, well, took you two long enough," joked Ralph.

Sarah snatched up her clothes that lay on the beach and quickly dressed. As everyone finished situating their clothes, they all tuned and enjoyed a laugh. It had been completely crazy, but in a way, it made them feel closer.

The five of them continued to joke about their midnight escapade in the sand as the guys walked Emily and Sarah back to their house. Ralph had brought a backpack with him, and it was not until he pulled out a shiny can that they realized it was full of alcohol.

"Anyone else care for one?" He opened the zipper wider, digging out four additional cans and passing them out. Sarah questioned herself but was open to anything that would ease her mind.

When they reached Sarah and Emily's, everyone came in to sit around, talking and drinking on the couch. The beach run seemed as if it was days ago now as they cracked the tab on another can.

When Ralph noticed his bag was empty, Sarah looked over at the clock on the wall. It was now two in the morning. "I think I am going to turn in for the night."

"Me too, Sar," said Emily.

"Well, ladies, it was fun," said Ralph as he got up to throw his can away. "So, an easy ten along the ocean front tomorrow?"

"Sounds good. Let's meet up at nine o'clock back at the beach."

With the next day's run planned, the guys walked back to their hotel, and Emily and Sarah got ready for bed. As Sarah lay down, she thought back on the night. She had never done anything so spontaneous. It felt weird, but a little freeing. Her mind continued to replay the run in her head as sleep evaded her....

The pain ran down the outside of her knee to her calf. The popping when she raised and lowered her leg was unmistakable. Like most injuries, this one lacked promise. The IT band was extremely tight, and could be only a few steps away from a tear. She ran her hand up and down along the side of her leg, trying to read her body....

She woke frantically, covered in sweat. Sarah looked over to see Emily in the bed next to her. It was 4 a.m. The dream had scared her for a second, believing the season was over just as it was beginning. As she lay back down and tried to fall back asleep, three words rose into her mind, *time and chance*. She tried to clear her thoughts, but the phrase lingered. It sounded familiar, but she couldn't place where she had heard it. Maybe it was because it was so late at night or so early in the morning rather. A sound pierced the stagnant silence of the room. Emily was talking in her sleep. *Oh, Emm*, she thought. With a quiet laugh, she lay back down and faded off to sleep.

CHAPTER 7:

Autumn

As the calendar turned to the first weekend of fall, the days continued with a summer heat, but the nights held a seasonal chill. In Beval, students wore shorts and breathable shirts while the sun shone. Then, as the mists of night cloaked the city, the transition to pants and light jackets was seamless.

Carrying on the yearly tradition, the team took a break from the excitement of the cross-country season to spend the latter hours of the day enjoying the town's annual fall festival.

Buffman's Farmhouse staged a majestic carnival that drew crowds from neighboring towns. The family had spent years as farmers, but when one season of devastated crops left them short on money, they had to make a choice: sell the land or come up with a way to make up the difference. As a result, Buffman's now housed the largest corn maze in the state, trails for hayrides, and a haunted house.

Paul had offered to pick up Emily, Sarah, and even Nigel. When he arrived, Nigel jumped into the back seat. With little regard, Sarah headed toward the passenger side while Emily climbed into the back. "Where is Ralph?" questioned Emily.

Ralph had recently taken up with Abby. Their relationship was kept hushed to avoid landing on Coach's radar. Although Cavlere supported co-ed fraternizing, dating and beyond was not condoned.

As Paul put it, "Ralph would be spending time alone with Abby tonight, so don't expect to see them at the farm."

Although Abby paced with another group of girls on the team, Sarah knew her well enough to infer she was likely working late, and Ralph stayed back to surprise her after a long day.

Pausing at the stop sign, Paul rolled down his window and turned on the radio to the local country station. Nigel's look of disgust indicated he wasn't a fan, but he was outnumbered by the other three. Attempting to drown out the music, Nigel leaned over the seat, letting down the passenger window. Sarah reached back to hold her hair as it flowed freely in the wind.

"Here, Sar," said Emily as she pulled a spare hair tie from her wrist. The tussle with the wind was clearly a loss, so Sarah pulled her hair back into a ponytail.

When the song that was playing came to an end, Sarah's ears jumped at hearing her favorite lyrics. The irresistible urge to sing faded with the awareness that her voice could be heard over the music.

"Wow, Sarah," said Paul. "That's pretty good."

Sarah blushed. She had only sung for others at church. On Sundays, however, she always avoided being the center of attention.

Nigel interrupted the awkwardness by unzipping his backpack. "I brought some roadies for us." He offered one to Emily, who declined in typical Emm fashion. Undeterred, he leaned over to give one to Paul.

"Dude, I have to drive."

"Ha, it is just the one," but Paul didn't take his hands off the wheel. Giving up on the others, "How about it, Sarah?"

"I am good, but thanks."

"Suit yourselves," he said popping the top of the can.

"You better finish that up quick, Nigel," demanded Emily. "They don't allow outside food or drinks, and no alcohol." Nigel obliged as he tilted the drink up until he polished off the rest.

"All done!" he yelled, as they made the final turn before the farm.

The gravel parking area overflowed with cars, so Paul opted for a spot along a ditch near the entrance.

"I have to hit a tree," Nigel exclaimed. Leaving him behind, Paul, followed by Sarah and Emily stopped by the ticket booth.

"Can I get three tickets?" Paul asked.

Sarah looked at Emily. Even though she'd rather he not pay for her ticket, Sarah lacked the will within herself to object. Emily, on the other hand, did not. "Um Paul, thanks, but we can get ours."

He turned around, looking at Emily then toward Sarah. Sarah just nodded in agreement.

"I know," he said, proceeding to purchase three tickets.

"Thank you, Paul, that was nice of you," offered Sarah.

"What about Nigel?" questioned Emily.

"What about him? He is not as cute as you two."

Sarah could feel her face blush red. Luckily, she was not facing Paul, or she would have been further embarrassed.

Emily rolled her eyes, followed with, "Not only is he fast, but he is a romantic too." Paul and Emily both laughed.

"So, what are we doing first? Besides waiting on Nigel to catch up."

"Let's take the hayride while the sun is still out. Then we can do the spooky corn maze and haunted house," suggested Emily.

"Sounds good, Emm," Paul replied.

"Thanks for waiting, guys," Nigel interrupted as he ran up to the group.

"You are just in time. We are going to hop on the wagon; it's unloading from the last ride."

The tractor sat idle as the previous group unloaded. Emily and Sarah steadied each other as they climbed aboard, using the stacked bales of hay as makeshift steps. With the girls sitting beside each other, Paul and Nigel were forced to share the bale across from them.

"Ah, y'all make a cute couple," grinned Emily.

"Alright, Emily, switch with me," said Nigel. "How am I supposed to get by with you moving?" he asked as the two pivoted from one foot to another.

"Crawl under me for all I care," said Emily. Nigel shook his head. Placing his hands under her armpits, he lifted her up, twisting around before sitting her down beside Paul.

A well-placed kick by Emily and Nigel would have been crawling on the floor. "Excuse me, Nigel?"

"You wanted by and you're too short to duck under."

There was no one else to join them, so the driver threw the bales below on the back. Placing one hand on the rear tire, he hoisted himself up on the tractor before releasing the throttle.

The old diesel trudged along the gravel path, leading to a dirt road just inside the woods. Nigel started telling them that monsters hid in the woods, waiting to jump out and snatch people as they passed by. Awaiting the climax, Paul poked Emily in her side. She jumped, giving a breathless scream and a well-deserved punch to Paul's arm. Settling down, Nigel attempted a similar scare tactic on Sarah. Instead of her sides, he attacked her shoulders, pulling her backward. Sarah's was caught off guard, rendering her helpless.

Instinctively, Paul lurched forward, grabbing her hand just before she fell over the side. Emily beat Sarah to the punch by smacking Nigel on the head. The blow did not deter him from continuing to laugh at Sarah's fear for her life.

The girls were silent after the jokes, only breaking as they realized the ride had gone longer than expected. "Paul how far is this thing supposed to take us? It's already getting dark."

"You got me. I thought it was just a twenty-minute ride, max."

"Hey!" Nigel yelled up to the driver, but the roar of the tractor muted his voice. "Guess we are stuck for a while."

As the sun sunk lower and the stars illuminated the sky, a chill rolled over the farm. Emily and Sarah settled down into the floor, hoping the surrounding hay would provide shelter from the wind. As the guys joined them, Nigel discretely placed his arm around Sarah, pulling her close enough to whisper in her ear.

"Sorry, Sarah." She had no reply for him, but the warmth he offered was welcoming. Setting aside the scare, she nestled in beside him. Emily shivered alone, her arms wrapped around her legs. Whether refusing to be outdone or from pure consideration, Paul cuddled closer to Emily. At first, his gesture was unwelcomed, but seeing Sarah and Nigel's coziness, Emily leaned her head back into his shoulder.

Silence persisted as the wagon crept along. They merely sat there enjoying the moment, until the tractor came to a stop at the farm. Paul checked his watch. "We probably have time for either the maze or the house before they close." he said.

Sarah and Emily looked at each other briefly as the smiles on their face confirmed they shared the same idea. They kicked off their boots and rolled their pants up above their calves, then took off running toward the maze. Paul started to chase after them, but Nigel stuck his arm out.

"Wait a minute; then, we will try and find them," he said.

Paul nodded and then started to unlace his boots. "I won't be able to catch them in these heavy things," he laughed.

As Emily and Sarah disappeared into the dark abyss, Nigel and Paul began running toward the maze. At the entrance, there were two paths. "You go one way and I will take the other," directed Nigel.

The corn maze was engulfed in a slight fog that settled in for the night. No lights illuminated the field from the perimeter, leaving the paths dim. Judging from the silence from within, they were likely the only ones inside.

Sarah ran as fast as she could without colliding with one of the corn-stalk walls, hindered additionally by the limited sight and bare feet. She took each turn waiting to be captured by the guys. She and Emily had split up and she saw no sign of her friend, making the surrounding stalks all the spookier as she wandered alone.

A loud shriek came from across the field. *Emily.* They had found her first. She sighed as she slowed to a walk. There was a vast amount of corn between them based on the noise. *I better try and find Emm now,* she thought. She continued to navigate through the paths toward Emily, but the winding course failed to wield her in that direction. She began to worry as she approached an intersection with four other trailheads. *Oh gosh, I am really going to be lost now.* As she stood there contemplating, she began to shiver. Goose bumps etched across her exposed calves. She contemplated calling out to the others, but she thought better of it, unwilling to admit her uneasiness.

As she started to step back toward the way she had come, an arm seized her waist as a hand clutched her mouth. She tried to scream, but she could only muster a muffled cry. Terror filled her body. The person was too strong for her to break away and run. She closed her eyes as she realized her efforts offered no escape. *What do I do now?* The man turned her face toward him, pulling her into his body. She could not see the stranger's face as her eyes fell short of his chin. His clasp engulfed her inferior body.

Her terror faltered; the chill that filled her body faded away as she found her head resting on his chest. The man lifted her chin, not exposing his identity. As she waited for something else to happen, he tilted his neck down, giving her a kiss on the forehead. The kiss felt good, right. Sarah arched her head back to gaze into the sparking eyes of her suitor.

"I got you," said Paul. She smiled and laid her head back on his chest.

A rustle in the stalks developed from nowhere, giving way to Nigel and Emily arguing.

"Oh wow! Sorry, y'all. Did we interrupt something?" joked Emily. Sarah pulled away, fighting embarrassment as Paul dropped his hands down by his side and into his pockets.

"Ah, Emm, I snuck up on Sarah and gave her a scare. I did not realize she was out here shivering," he said.

"Why are you cold, Sar? Come on, let's get you somewhere warmer." Emily tugged Sarah away, walking off in the direction her and Nigel had come. The guys followed behind them until the cover of the maze fell behind.

The four sought refuge near a roaring bonfire out in the open where a small crowd stood. Emily and Sarah took a seat, sharing a bale of hay, as Nigel continued to stand close to the fire.

"Where did Paul go?" asked Sarah.

"Not sure, he was right behind us."

"There he is, coming this way now."

Paul concentrated on the four cups, trying to prevent a spill. When he made his way back across the field, he handed each of them one. "Hot, homemade apple cider."

Sarah was the last to pick a cup. As she reached out, she could not help but smile at his generosity. Putting the rim up to her lips, the aroma filled her nostrils and seeped into her chest. She had loved cider ever since she was a child, and the seasonal drink remained one of her favorite fall delicacies.

The fire continued to roar long into the night after the rest of the attractions closed. Some people roasted marshmallows, while others caught sticks on fire. Sarah sat there looking into the flames and occasionally up at the night sky. Gazing into the ominous blanket sprinkled with stars brought on a chill that lingered just outside the grasp of the blaze.

"Did anyone get our shoes?" asked Sarah.

"Ha no. They are still down there. I will go get them though," said Emily. "Nigel, since Paul got the drinks, you can help me."

"There is always a catch with you, isn't there?" he asked.

"Yeah, now let's go before I make you do it by yourself." Once the two were out of earshot, Paul stood up.

"Want to go ahead and walk back to the truck?" Paul asked.

"Yeah sure, I should probably get home and get into some clean clothes."

They had parked just a short distance from where the fire was, making the barefoot walk across the gravel drive bearable. Instead of opening the doors, Paul let down the tailgate, and jumped up into the bed. Sarah looked at him for a second, as she knew she could not clear that height. Paul laughed, offering a hand to help her. Ignoring his gesture, she placed her hands on the tailgate. As she pushed herself off the ground, she swung her legs up, bring herself to her knees. With a smile, she turned around and sat down beside him.

"Well, well," he said.

"Don't underestimate me," she laughed.

"What do you think about those two?" said Paul pointing across the field.

"What do you mean?"

"Do you think they want to be alone? They just seem to be hitting it off."

"I think that's just Emily. Nigel doesn't really seem like her type."

"What about you then? Any interest in Nigel?"

"I haven't thought about it. He's nice looking; just not sure if he is my kind of guy."

"Oh, I got ya. I guess that can be difficult to tell with someone new that comes along." Then he blurted, "Who are you interested in anyways?"

For a second, she pondered over the question. In the past, a guy she was interested in had never asked her that. *Was he asking for Nigel, or for himself?* she wondered. She could not tell, and she was afraid to be as audacious as he was.

She worried, seeing Nigel and Emily returning with the bundle of shoes. Emily was laughing at something Nigel had said. They were moving closer and soon would be able to hear them. A feeling fogged her mind, a fleeting thought that this could be her only chance to express her honest feelings. She turned and looked at Paul, catching his eyes gazing at her. She started to speak. "You … wouldn't be interested," she broke away. She had tried but could not bring herself to speak out.

"Ah sure I would, but I get it, if you want to keep your secrets to yourself, then …"

"Shoe delivery!" yelled the two in unison as they threw the shoes into the bed of the truck.

"Were you two going to leave us here?" asked Emily.

"No, Emm, we just thought we would make our way back, ready to go when you came."

"Likely story," Emily replied.

"We had to walk through a mud pit to get these stinking shoes. Either that or walk around. Let's just say, Emily wanted to take the easier route," Nigel remarked.

"Glad you didn't lose a leg in there, Nigel. I would hate for you to lose a race on a technicality," Emily batted back.

Sarah was not paying attention; at this point, she was trying to crawl to the back of the truck bed to retrieve her shoes. She stretched out as far as possible to reach the shoelaces, but instead she slipped onto her stomach. The cold metal pressed up against her belly and chest. As she made a final try, she lunged out just enough to touch the laces. The stretch lifted the back of her shirt, exposing the small of her back to the night air. As she reached with her free hand to pull her shirt back down, Nigel called out, "Nice underwear."

She crawled back on her elbows until she was sitting on the tailgate. "Don't worry, it's nothing we haven't seen before," he continued. Any remaining pride from that night crumbled at the comment. She dropped down to the ground, silently walked to the passenger door, and climbed into the front seat. She could hear Emily defending her outside.

Paul followed her. "You okay?"

"Yeah, I will be fine," Sarah said shortly.

When Emily had finished with her lecture, they took their seats in the back.

"I'm sorry, Sarah, I was just kidding."

"It's fine, Nigel. I know."

Sarah rested her head on her hand with her elbow propped on the door. Refusing to dwell on the beach trip, she looked over toward Paul. He glanced at her from time to time as he drove them back to campus. The last time she looked over, he turned and smiled at her. She mustered a girlish grin.

CHAPTER 8:

The Marathon

October held the only open weekends during the racing season. Not to be confused, Coach directed them to maintain an easy run Saturday and a Sunday long run: thirteen miles for the girls, sixteen for the guys. As the season started, the girls and guys were expected to log closer to eighteen and twenty miles for long runs. An easy Saturday followed by a comparatively short Sunday lacked the needed drive for the middle of the season. Reluctant to ease up, Sarah decided to take a different approach to the weekend workout. In just a few months, she would be turning twenty-two. By that milestone in her life, she coveted the opportunity to complete a marathon.

One afternoon, Sarah had been flipping through the newspaper while waiting for Emily. She paused upon reading a race announcement for a marathon a few cities over. The timing matched perfectly with the open weekend. She thought about enlisting Emily to join, but knowing

Emily was more concerned with speed than distance, Sarah decided to go in it alone.

Standing alongside her car as the sun rose, Sarah looked out along the start of the course, visualizing how the day might go.

Click, the start of a timer, blasting off with a sense of explosion. Adrenaline releases from the pent-up nerves of the prolonged wait to start. The beginning would be easy. As the crowd of runners spread out, the stored energy subsides, and then she would find her stride.

Her plan was simple, but the lingering thought with every race was the acceptance of setbacks: maybe a mental block or something physical like a side stitch. No matter how well the race was going, she knew from the beginning how she wanted to finish: imagining coming across the finish line, seeing the exact paced time illuminated on the clock, and always stepping across the line in first.

Her high school coach broke races down into three stages. The first period was the beginning of the race where she would go out strong and fight for her spot. The second was meant to survive and keep pushing, and the third—that's where she would thrive.

Before the start of the marathon, Sarah jogged alongside the lake to warmup. A half mile would suffice if she kept her sweats on to help loosen the muscles. When moisture began gathering on her chest, Sarah switched to conducting her routine stretches. With her back to the car door she leaned over, touching her toes with her legs straight but not locked. Once this felt easy, she crossed her right leg over her left for the same time frame then switched. As she pulled away from her toes and to an upright position, she began working on her calves, hip flexors, and quads. When she finished all the standing poses, she opened her car door and pulled out a towel. Luckily, no rain had fallen, but she was unwilling to risk leaving marks on the back of the shorts. At practice, it was difficult to not flash someone during a team stretch. Sarah was always careful to be modest, even if she was wearing compression shorts or they had a lining.

A voice echoed over a bullhorn. "Five minutes until the start. All runners to the line!" Sarah checked the laces on her shoes and securely tucked them back underneath themselves. With one last sip of water, she locked her door and anxiously walked toward the crowd.

At the sound of a loud blast, they stormed off. Sarah pulled away from the slower runners and settled in at pace. Her strategy was to compete near a usual summer practice pace, then have about six miles of unexplored territory to push through. The day was forecasted to be warm for October, but with all the training for cross-country, Sarah doubted that would be a factor.

The course was outlined in stages. First, the group would ascend to the top of a mountain, then down one side, back up, down the other side, to the top once again, and then come down the front as they broke off to the finish. Based on the topography map and elevation chart, the climb was manageable. To reach the peak, each trail would cover roughly four miles, which based on the size of the mountain, was just a little more climbing than she was used to running at Dever.

The first eight miles flew by with ease. Coming up the front, a slight burn singed Sarah's leg muscles. However, the downward slope provided ample rest before climbing again. Before tuning at the bottom to begin her second ascent, Sarah sipped some Gatorade. She had never been accustomed to drinking or eating during a race, or even long runs. She might feel slightly dehydrated, but she always drank plenty of water beforehand.

Heading to the trailhead, Sarah looked around. She failed to notice any girls coming through, and only a few guys had passed her leaving the aid station as she came in. *What if I won my first marathon?* As a flame of determination lit, Sarah gained momentum.

By the time she got to the top and to the second aide station, the fire raged within. "You are almost half way there," one of the volunteers yelled. Her pace began to quicken. She checked her watch, one hour and twenty-five minutes.

She continued briskly for the next twenty-five minutes. The trail leveled out and the turnaround would be coming up soon.

An unwelcome urge she had experienced only a few times on a long run tightened her body. She had to pee. Peering about, no portables stood in sight. Again, no girls followed nearby, but at this point, a flock of guys still surrounded her. There was only one choice. The foliage was still thick on the trees, so she veered off the trail and found a tree well off the beaten path. She conducted a second check to insure no one could see her and then squatted down.

As she tried to rise, her leg muscles refused to budge from their locked position. A sharp pain traveled through her calves and thighs, limiting her gait. Worried, Sarah massaged the cramping muscles, hoping to dispel the lactic acid. She continued to walk until reaching the course and then slowly jogged until she could increase the pace. Shuffling another ten minutes brought no turn around. *Have I missed it? There are still other runners around. What's going on?*

She stopped. Mentally, she was broken. The energy she previously displayed was sucked from her legs, and the fire that raged within was extinguished. Shaking her head, Sarah tried to regain focus. She had never experience this before, and now she stood at a loss for what to do.

Checking her watch, a good five minutes had elapsed. The last mile marker she remembered seeing was sixteen, but that seemed forever ago. All she could force herself to manage was hobble. A stray tear trickled down her check. She wiped her face, trying to regain composure. She looked up at the sky in search of help.

The strain haltered her progression as she hunched over to brace her hands on her knees. "Everything okay over there?" asked two approaching guys.

"Yeah, at least I think so."

"Don't worry, you are still doing great. The next aide station is about a mile further."

Sarah silently groaned. "I am not sure if I can even do that," she replied; followed by the thought *And even if I can, how is that going to help?* The two guys persisted, offering to coach her along.

"Is this your first marathon?"

"Yeah; just struggling right now," she replied.

"That's alright," one of them assured. "We are going to slow it down for the next mile then regroup and refuel at the aid station. Try to hang with us until then. They have watermelon there; it will change your world."

"That does sound good," she said. Sarah managed to straighten her neck followed by her back.

"Just keep moving."

Promises of an aid station were not fulfilled for another eleven minutes. A group of ten others gathered around, refueling and restocking.

"Only one more aid station after this one, back on the top of the mountain and only a few miles from the finish."

Only a few runners took advantage of the watermelon, but John and Michael assured Sarah that she would feel much better if she ate some. There really was no other choice. She had tanked and was struggling to focus. Sarah picked up a chunk of the melon, one piece followed by a second. The luscious nectar hit her stomach, immediately restoring precious energy. The light switch flipped again; the darkness fleeing her sight. She picked up another slice.

John looked over, "See, I told ya. Just don't overdo it, or you will get a bellyache." Sarah nodded in agreement. She did not know if it was the rush of sugar or just having something to eat, but the wall that once stood in her way had vanished.

The three left the aid station and reestablished their pace. As they approached the base of the mountain, the two guys began to chat about the cookout they were having that night to celebrate. The talk of food kept Sarah's mind off the fact that her legs were getting heavier, but not her renewed craving for watermelon.

Until they reached the top, the group decided to break the run up into sections. For every five minutes of running, they would walk for a minute. Sarah appreciated the agreed upon plan, as she had wondered if summiting the top again was possible. *I just have to get to that final station; then it will be all downhill and into the finishing chute.*

It was not until Michael looked over at Sarah that anyone noticed. The skin on Sarah's face had passed from a red hue to a pale flush completion. "How are you feeling, Sarah?"

"I've been better, but we should be getting close." John and Michael exchanged a look of concern. Sarah barely caught their side-glance, but she knew something was not right.

"Yeah, we are; just keep pushing," they encouraged.

Reaching the final checkpoint, a subtle pain fixated in Sarah's knees. The downhill finish was not going to be kind to them either. There was just one way out of this race though, and the trail led the way. *It will be over soon*, she thought. After one final gulp of water, they turned to face the descent.

She could feel the adrenaline shooting through her veins. Her body garnered the strength for an extra push. They continued to accelerate as they churned down the trail, coasting back toward the lake. *Keep going,* she told herself. *Just another mile, okay, now anther mile.* Finally, she was splitting the remaining course into landmarks. *Okay, just got to get to that tree, now to the next turn.* The rush of adrenaline waning, time lost all relevance with each curve in the trail.

Rounding a corner, a roaring crowd echoed in the near distance. A small group was standing alongside a sign that read twenty-six. She had made it to the last mile marker.

John and Michael gave each other a high five then turned to Sarah. "Alright, let's bring it home!" They picked up their stride and started chanting with the group as they passed. The trail reached the head where the woods peeled back, and the sky emerged. They could see the lake now. All that was left was to cross the bridge then the finish line.

The two guys made a dash to the finish as they toed off from the bridge. Sarah kept her pace, only slowing as she neared the line, crossing with a slow gait, reading the illuminating red numbered timer. *Three hours and thirty-one minutes.*

Passing over the finish line, Sarah made her way to a nearby tree before collapsing on the ground. She laid her head on her knees, her arms hugging her legs.

"Here ya go, drink this."

"Thanks Michael," she said.

"Great time for your first marathon, Sarah, and not to mention you can qualify for some big name races with that kind of time," he said.

"Ha! It will be awhile before I can even think about running another race this distance."

"Ah. That's what everyone says, but then in a few weeks, you will be gearing up for the next one."

"Well, next week I have exams, so that's going to be on my mind first," she joked.

"Exams? What year are you?" he asked.

"I'm a senior, why?"

"That's just an insane feat for someone your age. Especially for a girl." The comment came almost as an insult, but she assumed he meant the remark in an encouraging way.

"Where do you go?" Michael asked.

"I am studying at Yemington, not too far from here."

"Oh yeah, we both went there. We must have just missed you though. We graduated four years ago. Is Jack still running the team over there?"

"He is," she said.

"I don't think he has any quit about him," he laughed.

"Thanks to both of you for pushing me through the race. I wasn't sure for a while how that was going to turn out."

"You did it on your own, but it was pretty apparent at one point that you were low on electrolytes. That's the tricky part about marathons, knowing to get in your nutrients before you need them. If you wait until you feel weak, recovery is a terror. Just make sure you take in some extra electrolytes today and tomorrow, or you are going to feel terrible," he advised and added, "By the way, we are having a party back at the house tonight, and you are welcome to come."

"I appreciate the invite, but I probably need to get some rest before I have to start studying," Sarah said as she shifted to get up from the ground.

"Easy, champ," exclaimed Michael as he offered her a hand. "Those legs of yours are going to feel weak, so be careful not to fall."

"Thanks. Would you mind helping me to my car? I rather not wipe out and hit the pavement."

Michael slid his arm around her waist and latched onto her side. Sarah leaned into him, using his shoulder for a brace. Together, they stumbled to her car. Opening the door for her, Michael helped ease Sarah down into the seat, hooking his arms under her shoulders, balancing nearly all her weight.

"Do you not have someone to give you a lift?" he asked.

"No, I didn't think it would be a big deal."

"Here, bring that towel and come sit out by the tree. The last thing you want to do is get behind the wheel." Sarah agreed to go back and meet up with John and some more of their friends.

"Here, I got you," Michael leaned over and picked her up, placing Sarah over his shoulder. She was not sure if she was more surprised in his ability to handle her after such a taxing race, or the fact that she was letting a stranger carry her. No matter, her exhaustion warranted her lack of care.

John and Michael carried the conversation of the group, as Sarah tried to listen. The daze that fogged her head insisted she flatten out on her stomach. She began to replay the race in her head. Considering the hundreds of miles ran this summer, this one instance left her more exhausted than ever before. As she rested her head on the ground, the chatter of the others drifted further away, until she finally fell asleep.

She awoke to Michael shaking her shoulder. "Wake up, Sarah. You've been asleep for an hour. We are all heading out now, but I didn't want to leave you lying here. You should be good to drive now."

Her tired eyes winced in embarrassment as she wiped a trail of slobber from her face. Michael's dimpled smile assured her that he understood.

When she arrived at her apartment, it was mid-day Saturday. Seeing Emily's car was gone, she decided to study for midterms. Picking up her math binder, she thumbed through her notes. The discussion in game theory had been centered on using what they had learned to create their own unique game. Sarah had slowly worked on the project over the past week, but tying in what she had been learning in ecology to a game was a daunting task.

There are two types of population growth curves, she read. Exponential growth, which can be shown as a J curve, or $e^{\wedge}x$, is for smaller organisms that reproduce at relatively fast rates. The population grows uncontrollably until the number of organisms explodes past what is referred to as caring capacity. Once this limit is broken, a massive dying off occurs in the group, causing the total population to plummet. Then the cycle repeats.

The other is sigmoidal growth, or what many mathematicians refer to as an S curve. The growth pattern here starts much like exponential growth. However, there is a point on the curve, called the point of inflection, where on the graph of the population the line actual curves back the other direction, forming an S shape. The group does continue to grow, yet as they approach carrying capacity, the curve flattens out, just like a graph reaching a limit.

The thought she had been focused on was centered around the sigmoidal graph. This group appeared to face a game of survival at the point of inflection and at the carrying capacity, but neither point in time appeared much of a game. *Maybe the group adjusts to the environment instead*, she thought. The exponential growth, however, displayed an obvious game of chance. Once carrying capacity was reached, all of the individuals must compete for resources.

Sarah had been pondering over this idea, but she was unsure how to mathematically prove that logistical growth is likely not a game of chance, whereas exponential growth was. Sarah's eyes blinked slowly as she looked over her notes, searching for a solution. The quick nap she had after the race wasn't enough. Deciding to sleep on her query for now, she lay down in her bed to try to recover from the race.

The slamming of the front door announced Emily's return home. Sarah stretched her legs and arms outward while yawning. A setting sun now filled the sky. *That's crazy. I must have slept pretty hard. Wait that's it, crazy or chaos. What if I used something to display chaos in the proof?*

"Sarah, where are you?"

"I'm in my room." She could hear Emily running up the stairs just before her door flew open.

"Hey, why are you in bed so early?"

"I just got back from a race and crashed," she grinned. Emily's curious face lightened as Sarah proceeded to tell her everything that happened and the two guys that helped her finish. Concluding the story by reen-acting her slobbery awakening, Sarah packed up her backpack and drove to the library.

CHAPTER 9:

Midterms

By Thursday afternoon, Sarah had finished her three midterms and her game theory presentation. Coming back from the marathon and trying to cram in studying had called for a few late nights. On Tuesday, she stayed at the library past two in the morning. The ecology test, which she thought would be easy, had been left for the last possible second to prepare for.

Emily dropped her pencil posing a hint of frustration. "Sarah, I need coffee," she protested.

"Do you want to go downstairs with me?" Needing a break, Sarah took her up on the offer to join. Pacified, Emily stayed with Sarah a few more hours before calling it a night and deciding to drive home.

"Are you sure you want to stay? I can crash on a couch in the corner and wait on you if you like."

"That's alright; I have some more labs to review for the free response, but I want to look over them all," Sarah insisted.

"Okay, but don't come wandering in at six tomorrow morning," Emily laughed.

After the farewell, Sarah turned back to her notes.

The jerking of her neck later confirmed she was nodding off. Realizing she had not accomplished anything for a good forty minutes, Sarah decided to leave the library. Throughout the semester, she had an A in all her classes, but now there was doubt that hung in her hopes.

Sarah looked around as she gathered her belongings. There were a few students still working, while others appeared to be dallying. As she headed toward the door, she noticed Paul sitting alone, staring blankly out the windows.

"How is the studying going?" she asked.

"I think I am done," he replied, looking at his watch as he shuffled his notes to pack up. "Did you drive over?"

"No, I took my bike," she answered. "I guess I wasn't planning on staying so late."

"You can put your bike in the back of my truck, and I will take you back," he offered.

"You don't have to do that," she replied.

"Nonsense; I know it's a safe town, but I wouldn't feel right letting you wander alone in the dark," he said.

Sarah smiled slightly. "If you don't mind, that would be great. I know Emily worries when I do that."

The two of them walked down the stairs, chatting softly to the back of the library and into the parking lot. Clutching Sarah's bike, Paul proceeded to open the door for her, and single-handedly hoisted the bike, placing it in the bed of the truck. As Sarah pulled on the seatbelt, she recalled the last time they rode alone in his truck. It had been about a year ago since what had been a night of two friends going out. She had been skeptical, as it had felt more like a date.

Paul opened the door, and stuck his head in. "Are you hungry?"

"Humm… maybe a little now that you mention it," she said.

"Great! I am starved. How about we get a late night snack in the dining hall?"

"I would be alright with that," she said.

The dining commons' main corridor closed at ten, but there was a small section of the kitchen and a sitting area that remained open all night. Usually, a few people studying or perhaps returning from a bar wandered in throughout the night.

Paul ordered a double decker burger while Sarah settled on a bowl of cereal. Sitting down across the table from Sarah, Paul started to laugh. "What is so funny?" she asked.

"You don't seem like an after-hours type of girl," he said.

She grinned, "Well I'm not, Paul. Like my mama always told me, if you are out past eleven, steer clear of trouble."

"That sounds like a good rule to live by. I guess that means I am not troubling you," he laughed.

"Not at all; quite the opposite."

"We should do this more often," Paul suggested.

"What do you mean?" asked Sarah.

"Go out for a meal, or coffee, before eleven, of course. You know, change things up from time to time."

"Oh, with the team?" asked Sarah.

Paul's eyes faded back down toward his burger. "Yeah with the team for sure." He took an oversized bite, provoking a period of silence to follow.

The burning grease aroma dissipated as the dinner area cleared out. Soon, they were the only ones left. As Sarah spooned up the remainder of her milk, and Paul dipped the last few fries, the beep of Paul's watch pierced the air.

"Wow, it's already four o'clock," he said.

"Eek, I told Emily I would be back before six." Their laughter carried, echoing off the far wall.

"In that case, we better get going. I would hate to go against Emm's wishes."

Steam clouded the tray drop off as the washer bellowed from behind the window. Paul stacked Sarah's tray on top of his and placed them in the chute as she waited for him at the door. Entering the night air, Paul took Sarah's hand. Although briefly, as the walk was not far, there was a satisfying moment that accompanied the gesture.

Arriving at Sarah's, Paul put the truck in park and looked over at her. "Thanks for joining me. That made for an interesting night."

"Yeah, it was fun; I just hope my ten o'clock exam goes well now," she replied with a half grimace and half smirk. Paul looked back to his door and stepped out of his truck walking around to retrieve Sarah's bike.

"Thanks again," said Paul as he leaned in and gave Sarah a hug. A hug that lingered in a warm and welcoming way. Sarah took in a deep breath and began to pull away.

"Any time, Paul." She walked to the door and waved bye before turning the key.

Quietly, Sarah snuck upstairs, trying not to alert Emily. Dropping her backpack by the door, she turned and went into her bathroom. Hastily, she brushed her teeth and washed her face before changing into a pair of pajamas.

A glowing 4:23 showed on the clock dial. She would need to be up by nine to make it to class. Before getting into bed, she checked to see if Emily was awake, but her friend had long been asleep; otherwise, Emily would have heard Sarah and immediately questioned the late return. Before laying her head on her pillow, Sarah set her alarm and said her prayers. It wasn't long once she had settled in her comfortable covers that she drifted off to a final thought of eating with Paul.

The delayed alarm jerked Sarah awake. Instead of setting the alarm for nine, she mistakenly set it for nine thirty. Despite worries of missing the test, it proved advantageous. Taking a seat minutes before testing commenced, there was no drowsiness as she expected.

Midway, the lack of sleep had overpowered this rush. Despite her focus draining, Sarah pushed her way through the exam but was left no time for a break as she headed straight to the Boyd basement. All tutors were required to work a minimum of two hours during exam week. Despite its unalluring mystique, the lounge promised frantic students pleading for help upon the eve of withdrawal deadlines. Additionally, after work, her project would require the final touches, as Thursday was set aside for presenting their game theory projects in lieu of midterms. This alternative took some pressure off, as Sarah had taken time to prepare over the past few weeks.

CHAPTER 10:

The Question

"Sarah, you are up next," Professor Strom called out.

Stepping up to the front, Sarah placed her notes and hands on the wooden podium. Tucking her hair back behind her glasses, she positioned the frames on the bridge of her nose. Her black skirt and gray blouse were the usual combination she wore for the rare instances she had to address an audience. She gathered her notes as she turned on the overhead projector to display her graphs on the board.

"Good morning, everyone," Sarah began. "I have prepared a discussion on the topic of population growth patterns and how they affect the chances of survival. It is important to note that the exponential curve represents organisms that have short life spans and reproduce at high rates, like bacteria. The logistical curve is a representation of organisms that have relatively longer life spans with lengthier reproduction cycles, yielding less progeny. Humans would be included in this group. Comparing the two types, we can see how one set of individuals levels off before surpassing the upper limit known as the carrying capacity. The J-shaped curve, however, expands without bounds until a threat to survival occurs. The theory that I have stems around how at a certain point, the two graphs begin to change from looking similar to one diverging from its original trajectory. In general, when you evaluated the two types, this appears to happen at the point of inflection. Consider a few knowns. There are two populations, R and K. R-selected is a group of simple organisms that show exponential growth, and K-selected is a group of complex individuals that show sigmoidal growth. R individuals are found in unstable environments, where K organisms are found in stable environments.

"What I am postulating is that there is no game of chance for population K species that occupy the same space and resources; however, there is for the R population. To evaluate this mathematically, I used the Nash Arbitration Scheme. John Nash states if you graph the function $y=x$, anything over this line is considered unstable. If we evaluate the two graphs at the beginning, say at time $t1$, they are similar as both fall under the line $y=x$. However, by evaluating the two graphs after the point of inflection, we see that the r-selected organism's population sky-rockets past the line we created, but the K-selected group curves underneath the line. This confirms that the S-curve graph is a representation of a stable population, which would develop in a stable environment. Therefore, competition is low.

"The R group is much different. Since the J curve rises above $y=x$, the environment must be unstable. Such turmoil leaves us to derive that there is a reason for chaos to occur due to increased competition as the population soars toward and ultimately above carrying capacity.

"To sum up, the J curve is not stable after a given time, whereas the S curve is. My conjecture for this project: based on the chance of competition, R-selected organism can experience periods of competition, whereas K-selected organisms cannot."

Looking around the room, most of the stares consisted of blank faces. "Are there any questions?" she asked.

When she turned toward the professor, he had an inquisitive look about his face. "I like your postulation; however, there seems to be more needed to further fill this conjecture. I'm no biologist, so it is hard to say if there were any missing steps after you built your main case. However, I must say I enjoyed your take on trying to apply game theory to ecology," he said.

All eyes in the class fell on her, casting a shade of disbelief and humiliation. She had taken a chance, proposing a scientific insight and explained it mathematically, yet the message did not resonate. Sarah gathered her notes and took a seat at her desk.

"Okay, class, who is next?" the professor asked.

Nigel raised his hand. "Let's go, Mr. Branan. You're up."

For the next twenty minutes, Nigel discussed a presentation on the game Mancala. On the projector, he wrote out a strategy designed to win the game. Everyone's focus was captured by his presentation, to the point he even engaged the professor.

When class was dismissed, Sarah did not linger but headed straight to the door. Walking down the hall and finally to the stairs, a voice called out to her. It was Nigel. "Hey, Sar, wait up."

She paused.

"That was a pretty profound presentation you gave there. Just from what I know, that could be a huge insight if you finalized your conjecture into a theory," he said.

"Thanks, Nigel. I am not sure that was the impression the teacher got, but I was definitely going for something along those lines."

"Where are you headed now?" he asked.

"I am going to get something to eat and then try to take a nap before practice. How about you?"

"I have my last midterm. What are you doing after practice today? What do you say I pick you up and we have dinner?"

Sarah blinked a few times, allowing her brain to catch up to his final question. On the spot, she did not have plans and could not fabricate an excuse.

"Dinner; yeah sure, I could do that."

"Awesome; I will swing by around seven." With that confirmation, he cut to the left and was gone.

CHAPTER 11:

A Date

S arah stood in front of the mirror, brushing her teeth. The week had not gone as planned regarding her exams and project, and now she was going out with Nigel. She almost called off the date but decided otherwise at the last minute. As she stared back at her reflection, a lingering thought filtered through her mind. *What about Paul? We had an amazing night together after the library, but he didn't ask me out.* Sarah was a little perplexed. *One date with Nigel can't hurt. Then, when nothing more comes out of tonight, Paul might come around.*

About that time, Emily walked into the bathroom. "Wow, Sar you look amazing. I bet your boy thinks so too."

"He isn't my boy anything. I just want to look nice," Sarah said.

Sarah had decided to pull out her favorite fall dress with a sweater for the date. It was a plain, dusty orange, knee-length, shoulder-cusped dress that complemented her skin tone well.

The day after Sarah's long night out with Paul, Emily asked her when she had ended her studying. Sarah admitted it was late, but that she could not remember because Paul and she had been hungry, stopping for a quick bite at the dining hall. Her explanation had not been fully truthful as she made the late night seem more casual than she honestly believed. She did let Emily know Paul was sweet enough to drive her back, so she did not ride home in the dark. When Emily questioned if she had any interest in Paul, Sarah had not denied it, but simply suggested a maybe.

Emily must have known Sarah was contemplating something as she fished through her thoughts. "Are you nervous? Do you think Paul will mind you two are going out?"

Sarah blushed. "I am not nervous, but I do wonder if I should be going out with Nigel when there could be something with Paul."

"That's what dating is for," said Emily. "If you don't like one, then see what happens with the other. You're a sweet girl; that's all anyone can ask of you."

"Thanks, Emm. I don't mean to change the subject, but do you mind if I borrow your diamond earrings?"

"Fancy evening?" teased Emily. "Only joking; I know you love wearing them any time you get a chance."

Sarah knew the earrings were the only heirloom Emily received from her grandmother, but Emily was proud to lend them to her.

As Emily returned with the earrings, the two heard a noise from outside. "Can you see if that is him?" asked Sarah. Emily went over to the window to peer outside.

"No; it is just our neighbors causing a commotion. What time is he supposed to be here?"

"He said seven," Sarah said and looked down to check her watch; it was five 'til already. She hurriedly went to the closest to find a pair of flats that went with the rest of her outfit. Picking the shoes out from the closest, she sat them by the door.

"What is the plan for tonight, Sarah?"

"I am not really sure; he didn't say much. Just that he asked me to go out tonight. So probably dinner, then maybe walk around and talk."

The two sat down beside each other. Sarah ran her hand along her legs. She had shaved right before practice, as she knew she would be pressed for time. She was agile enough to run a razor hastily over them without nicking her skin, but the last thing she wanted was to conceal a cut or stop the bleeding.

"I will be in my room studying, Sarah, unless I need to leave," said Emily jokingly.

"Hardly! I am not going to invite him in. We know each other, but I'd rather not send the wrong message. He seems nice enough, but he has to earn some trust from me if he wants to date."

Emily looked up and noticed the skies darkening. "What time is it now, Sarah?"

"I guess he is running a little late," she replied.

"Did you see him and Paul today at practice?"

"Yeah, I did; it looked like they were not happy. What do you think that was about?"

"I guess they are frustrated all the time from racing and practice, so they haven't contemplated being friends," Emily said. "Don't you think?"

Another ten minutes passed before they heard a honk from outside. Getting up, Emily went to open the door. "Oh my!" she exclaimed.

Walking over, Sarah met her outside. Nigel was straddling his bike, motioning to her. Cutting the engine off, he flipped open his helmet cover and reached for a spare helmet from behind. Sarah and Emily exchanged concerned looks.

"Emm, I can't go out wearing this on his bike."

Sarah excused herself and ran back into her room. Shedding her dress, she threw it to the side of her bed. Quickly, she pulled out a pair of jeans and a green long-sleeved shirt she thought would not flap around in the wind. She placed each leg into the pants and pulled them up past her knees then to her waist. Buttoning the jeans closed, she looked up in the mirror. Her bra went particularly with the dress she had on. She turned to her wardrobe, snatched one of her regulars from the drawer, and pinched the hook on her back. Hurriedly, she switched out the two undergarments. Once she had her shirt pulled over her head, Sarah snatched her tennis shoes and a jacket before heading downstairs.

She tried to stop at the door briefly to regain her composure before going outside.

"Have fun," whispered Emily, giving her a hug. Turning from Emm, Sarah walked up to Nigel, hiding her frantic state the best she could.

"Hey," she said as he handed her the helmet.

"You ready?" She shook her head as she buckled the strap around her chin. Gingerly, she balanced herself on his shoulder as she stepped up, sliding her leg to the other side of the bike.

Soon, Nigel was riding toward his house. Sarah was not sure why he needed to stop there, only curious. "This will only take a minute; come in and wait," he said. Once Nigel opened the door, Sarah stepped into a rather dank house decorated with mismatching furniture and lewd posters. "Care for a drink?" Nigel asked.

"No thanks," she replied. Turning, he went up the stairs, taking them two at a time.

The living room was messy but nothing Sarah assumed was out of the ordinary for college guys. A foreign stench pierced the air, possibly the garbage that needed taking out. To the side of the kitchen, there was a couch and a coffee table. Lying bunched up on the sofa was a pink sorority sweatshirt. On the table sat an ashtray with two buds, one with pink lipstick.

She stopped staring as Nigel came walking down the stairs. "Sorry about the mess. My roommates tend to leave their stuff everywhere."

"Oh, that is alright." He noticed her still eyeing the coffee table.

"Do your roommates smoke?"

"Yeah, they do." Feeling at ease, Sarah turned toward the door and was followed out by Nigel. "I thought we could take my car since it is dark." Nigel opened the door of his red Camaro to let Sarah in. He offered his hand as she swooped down into the front passenger seat. He looked down at her as she buckled her seatbelt.

"What?" she laughed. Arching his head inside, he leaned over, kissing Sarah softly on the lips. She smiled as he stood back up. Shutting the door, Nigel walked to the other side and started the car. Sarah sank down into her seat, admitting to herself the date had been a good idea.

CHAPTER 12:

Something New

"For today, we are going to work on your speed with 400 meter intervals," Coach said. "The object of this is to stay at race pace. Guys, you will have twenty-four and girls sixteen. But, first, I want everyone to do a three-mile warm up. To finish off, you will have a two-mile cool down."

They nodded in agreement.

As of this week, they would max on their speed workouts for the season, only to hold this system of workouts until region. The top guys and girls would advance to nationals, yet the others would not call it a season. Coach had always practiced the method of, "You train every year as if you were going all the way. Then your body will be accustomed to the load once you make that jump to the big stage."

After Coach concluded his speech, Sarah bent down to retie her loose laces. As she rose back up, everyone had left to begin the three-mile portion of practice. She could see Emily up ahead nearing the trail while talking to Paul. As Sarah stepped out, Nigel came running through the parking lot, zig zagging between cars. "Let's go, slow poke!"

"I'm coming; I just had to fix my ... never mind."

"Sure, that's what they all say."

The two continued to run as they took up with the back of the pack. "Sarah, I am having a party, and I think you should come."

She thought for a second. The date they had the other night had gone off well, but the two had not spoken since. She was not sure if this was a friendly invite or another date.

"No pressure, though," he followed up. And just as she was trying to think of how to respond, Emily finally noticed her absence.

"Sarah, what are you doing in the back?" she yelled.

"Um, can I bring Emily with me?" Sarah asked.

"Sure thing; I haven't gotten to everyone yet, but I figure I will be asking the team to come. Just didn't want to get a lecture from Coach if I made a big announcement," he laughed.

"Alright," she agreed. Sarah picked up the pace, and with Nigel following, they made their way to Paul and Emily.

Returning from the out and back, the team gathered around in a circle to stretch out before the speed workout.

"Okay. Everyone, the idea here is to hit your four hundreds at your goal race pace. I have talked with each of you over the week about what we expect for each of you to achieve. That said, I have given everyone a split to memorize. I want you to eat, sleep, dream, and study that time. If you go slower, I want you to make up for it on the next rep. Likewise, if you are faster, you will have to slow it down. I want your bodies to get familiar with this pace. In between each set, you will have one minute of rest. However, you are not to stop. That means no standing around, no walking—only jogging, then back on the line. Once you have completed the last four hundred, you will group off to complete your two-mile post-workout. Any questions?" The group fell silent. "Okay then, let's go!"

At the sound of the whistle, the team took off in waves. Nigel and Paul were in the front and Sarah and Emily fell right in the mix of the other guys. At first, there was some bumping and squirming before the team started to spread out. As each person came around the track, they called out their times to Coach. "Alright, alright, keep moving and make your adjustments if needed on this next lap.

Lap after lap, the team started off true to their times. Sweat began to stream down their faces. Each lap they would sip some water, only swallowing enough to quench their thirst. By laps thirteen and fourteen, a few of the girls and one of the guys were noticeably struggling. It wasn't until the fifteenth lap that coach pulled those girls from the track; Peter was taken off at lap twenty-one. They were freshman. However, those freshmen did not warrant Sarah's attention. Abby's preselected splits were set short of Sarah's pace, but the grit outlining Abby's face sounded her rebellion. Coach said nothing as she continually bettered each time.

Sarah could remember her first year on the team when they had reached this week during the season. It was a true indicator of who had the stamina to handle the pressure of performing well at region. Even now, Sarah could feel the strain of the repeats. Her focus had dwindled from obtaining her own splits to staying close to Emily, who was having her own struggles with the workout. Still, the two pushed together, keeping close enough to their given marks for Coach to only grumble under his breath at the falter. Sticking to the plan, they transitioned after their final lap to the cool down without discussion. Doing so, Sarah could feel her body adjusting as the sweat began drenching her shirt.

Arriving back at the cars, Sarah ran her arm across her forehead to wipe the remaining sweat from her face, cringing at a peculiar smell. *Is that coming from me?* she thought. Discreetly, she tucked her nose to her shoulder imitating a scratch to check her underarm. She had encountered this scent somewhere before … With a second inspection, Sarah recognized the pungency of ammonia. Trying to avoid capturing everyone's attention, she backed away toward the edge of the group and bent down to loosen her laces. To mask the aroma, she removed her socks and shoes, wedging them just below her armpits. Still, Sarah was not fully convinced the cover was working. Forgoing the team stretch, she sat alongside the car waiting until Emily was done. Only when they were inside and Emily made no mention of the smell was Sarah able to relax.

When the car came to a stop outside their apartment, Sarah left Emily talking with the neighbors as she hurried to the bathroom and stripped down. Placing her sports bra to her face, she could still smell the ammonia. Picking up her shorts from the floor, she sniffed them to discover the same. Tossing the clothes back to the ground, Sarah reached under the sink for a towel and stepped into the shower. She lathered head to toe until a thick coating of suds formed. *That was so embarrassing. What if Emily noticed, or worse, if one of the guys caught a whiff?* After scrubbing down, she stood under the steaming waterfall to drain away the filth.

The last of the water dripped from the showerhead as she wrapped a towel around and eased from the tub. She balled up the running clothes and threw them in the washing machine. Only a few other articles needed cleaning, but she inspected each before adding them to the laundry. The bras and shorts only emitted the normal body odor after a long practice. With a twist of clicks, the knob directed toward the small load indicator and was left to swash.

The humiliation cornered Sarah back in the bathroom. She needed something in case this happened again. Inside a pull-out drawer, a half-used deodorant stick sat behind her toothbrush. Once dressed, Sarah walked downstairs to retrieve her gym bag from the car.

"Oh, Sar, you left your shoes in the car, so I grabbed them for you. They're over by the door so they can air out for tomorrow." Sarah's eyes widened in horror. "Everything okay?"

"Yeah, of course; I just thought you were going to say I left my shoes at the track."

Walking by, Emily reached her hand out to Sarah's arm. The bra strap had slid off Sarah's shoulder. "Your new bra needs adjusting," pointed out Emily.

"Oh, this one isn't…" she began, but Emily had already made her way up the stairs.

Closing the door behind her, Sarah bent down to inspect the insoles. She wasn't sure if it was just her imagination, but she thought there was a trace of ammonia. The regular shoe smell seemed to overpower anything else and Emily had not questioned their odor, so she peeled back the tongues before returning inside.

Sarah knew she needed to dedicate more time for studying. Her midterm score postings were less than encouraging. The hopes for As now dwindled to desperation for Bs or possibly Cs. The harsh reality was iced with regret for telling Nigel she would attend the party. The weekends would serve as prime time for the extra studying she needed without sacrificing sleep. *As long as Emily goes, though, it should be fine. We can stay an hour then head home.*

Sitting down at her desk, Sarah opened her abstract algebra notes. They had been discussing a ring within a field. All the rules had fastened into an intricate system. The thought process made sense, yet creating proofs was not easy. *Just remember, you can find a ring within a field,* she read. Going further with this concept, every field is indeed a ring.

However, every ring is not a field. Let's put this into a conditional statement. If a ring is a field, then a field is a ring. This statement would be true given our previous statement. The converse, if a field is a ring, then a ring is a field, is not necessarily true. The conclusion of the condition might be true or false. The biconditional statement, a ring is a field if and only if a field is a ring, therefore, would have to be false; remember from when we discussed truth tables? So, a ring is a set of numbers that satisfies certain properties you would see with addition and multiplication, such as being communitive and associative. The field, however, throws in another operation, division, with certain parameters that must be met. Sarah's notes came to a stop, as they were to discuss those terms in depth the next class.

She was not sure why they were called rings and fields, but the important piece was she needed to know how to determine if a set of numbers was a ring, a field, or both.

A yell from Emily interrupted her concentration. "Hey, Sarah, do you want to ride with me to dinner?"

"I would, but I need to spend time on this homework."

"Alright, so maybe I will see you there in a bit?" Emily said.

"Yeah; I will be along shortly."

Revisiting the paper, she began working through the problems, evaluating sets. The laborious task required perfection or the whole problem would be rendered incorrect.

A slamming of the front door sometime later recalled Sarah's lapse in joining Emily for dinner. "Hey, Sarah, are you still studying?" Emily inquired.

"Yeah; I'm so sorry. I forgot to take a break," Sarah said, looking at her watch, noting that the hour was about to switch from nine to ten.

"Do you want me to go with you to get something?"

"No; I think I will just grab a snack and head to bed. We have to be up early for our morning run tomorrow."

"Oh, yeah! I almost forgot about that."

"Hey, Emm, Nigel invited us to a party he is having. I told him I would come only if you would. What do you think?"

"Sure. That sounds fun."

Shutting her book, Sarah decided to forgo the snack. Instead, she shed her clothes, tossing them into the hamper. From the closet, she changed into an oversized shirt and a pair of boxers. Unhooking her bra, she laid it aside for the next day. She glanced at the mirror in front of the bed. Running her hand along the waistband, the elastic felt loose. The reflection showed no prominent changes, but the low riding boxers only provided confirmation of what she suspected. Dismissing the thought, Sarah placed the baggy T-shirt over her head and pulled her hair from the hole, allowing it to cascade down her back. The wrinkleless bed covers peeled from their fitted position with a slight tug. Each of Sarah's feet settled into a warm pocket to aid her sleep after the whisper of a prayer.

The next morning, rain beat along the roof and speckled the windows. A harsh glow from the nightstand clock foretold the impending alarm. Trying to fight the temptation to roll over and fall back asleep, Sarah emerged from the sheets instead of succumbing to a continued restless snooze. Heading to the bathroom, she looked at the calendar to confirm it was a Wednesday, but her eye was caught by the date below, circled in red. After washing her face, Sarah changed into her running shorts and went to check if Emily was awake.

Today, they had four miles for the morning run. With the dark gloom brought on by the rain, Coach would assign the team parking deck duty. Given his hardened core for running, Cavlere always held their best interests at heart. However, practice would continue, as scheduled, along the winding tracks of the damp corridors.

Removing their raincoat hoods as they arrived at the gym, Sarah noticed that a few faces were missing. Coach's façade foretold his frustration. Rain, sleet, and snow were no excuses to miss a practice, and five teammates had failed to show. The ones who braved the journey gathered around, stretching until coach signaled and they headed to the parking deck.

The wind jostled in resistance, spraying rain through the open doors and onto the tile floor. Despite a brisk jog to the deck, the puddles and rain left shoes and socks saturated. The smooth concrete was slick under their soles. Although conditions were better under the slabs, a sharp cut by Ralph on an inside corner swept his feet from beneath him. His elbow skidded the ground, scraping the skin. Through the remainder of the run, a dotted trail of blood dripped from his arm and marked a trail on the porous surface.

A fresh clot bandaged the wound by the time they arrived back at the locker rooms. To greet them, a heated letter was plastered on each locker. The fiery words advised the whole team was required at morning practices.

"This will be the one and only warning for the entire body. For those who skip practice unexcused again, they will find themselves removed from racing the rest of the season, regardless of position on the team."

The rest of the day, sheets of rain pelted the ground continuously over the campus. Despite the cruel lure to crawl back into bed, Sarah spent the remainder of the day either in class or nestled in a nook at the library. She stopped by the coffee shop for a cup of steaming light roast. The thoughts of the damp morning faded with the soothing drink. Even the rain streaming down the windowpanes of the library had no effect.

CHAPTER 13:

The Party

A gust rattled past the window, shaking a few gleaming yellow and orange leaves from the branches. The setting sun cast sharp hues reflecting off the trees, indicating the peak of autumn was near. Pumpkins carved with ghastly faces and spooky characters adorned the doorsteps of all the neighboring apartments in preparation for Halloween.

Emily was finishing her hair in the bathroom while Sarah pulled her orange and black socks up her calves. Clutching a pair of shoes, Sarah called out, "I am ready when you are," as she walked into her bathroom.

"Alright, just trying to get this knot out of my hair," said Emily.

On the counter lay the hair tie she had forgotten to return to Emily.

"Hey, Emm…," but before she finished, she rolled the band over her wrist. A lone hair on her eyebrow had caught her attention. Pinching the hair between her nails, she gave a quick jerk.

"All done, Sar; let's go. I can drive if you like."

"Actually, the weather is supposed to be nice and his house is not far. How about we walk?"

"That would be lovely. Maybe we can convince Paul to drop us off," smirked Emily.

The moon had risen in full phase and the stars' faint glimmer dusted the sky. As the two walked along, the buzzing of street lamps accompanied them. "Do you know who all is coming Sarah?"

"He said he was inviting the team."

"Oh fun! Ralph is always the life of the party, so we will be entertained to say the least." Making their way to the bottom of the hill, they turned toward Nigel's. Just out of sight, blue lights flickered as the campus police made a traffic stop. "Another good reason to walk," Emily bantered.

Even though they were only a few blocks from the party, the bass of the music carried down the road. A few excited screams and yells could be heard above the beat. Checking her watch, Sarah saw that the time was a little past eight. "He said any time after eight, so we are really just fashionably late if anything."

Finding their footsteps down the dimly lit walkway, they stood at the door for a moment before knocking. A few soft raps later, there was no answer. As Emily reached to turn the knob, the door flung open. It was Nigel.

"There you two are. Come in, come in." As Emily walked through, Nigel caught Sarah at the door with a peck on the lips.

Still, smoke laced with numerous stenches fogged the living room of Nigel's house. Chants followed by drowning roars and cheers pulsated to the vibrant background music. Rooms spilled over with students following a game or dancing to the beat. In the corner sat a love seat crammed with two couples, including Ralph and Abby. Sarah could not make out their conversation, but Ralph soon stood up, leaving Abby stirring silently in fury.

Emily followed Nigel into the kitchen, but Sarah broke away toward the living room. "Hey, Abby. What's wrong?"

Wiping her face with a sleeve, Abby choked up at she tried to regain her composure. "I told Ralph I cannot stay late, but he just said he couldn't make any promises. Then we started arguing. We haven't had a fight yet and ...."

Sarah reached over to give Abby a hug. "That's alright; it happens to the best of relationships. Come talk with Emm and me. We can walk you back when we leave."

"Thanks, Sarah; I would appreciate it." Abby laughed. "I really like Ralph, but he, well, you know."

Sarah smiled. "I get what you mean." Getting to her feet, Sarah reached out for Abby's hand. "Come on, let's go find Emily."

The group had settled around the countertop in the kitchen. Emily was talking with Paul and Nigel as Ralph fumbled with a cap. "Let me get you two a drink," said Nigel as he reached into the fridge, retrieving two bottles.

"Here ya go," yelled Ralph, handing them a set of keys with a bottle opener attached to the chain. Clicking the glass together, Ralph let out a "Cheers!" that could be heard across the room.

Looking about the house, Sarah noticed many unfamiliar faces. In fact, aside from her and the five others, she did not recognize anyone else. On the far wall, the door swung open. On the back porch was a keg in a tub filled halfway with ice. Two guys were flirting with a girl with curly black hair wearing a purple sweater and black pants. Both guys were laughing and gesturing with their hands, imitating doing pull ups. The girl had been unconvinced so far; however, she finally caved to their insistence. Placing the hose into her mouth, steadying her hands on the rim of the keg and lacing her fingers through the handles, she nodded her head. Together, both men bent over, grabbed her legs and hoisted them straight into the air. If not for one of the guys holding the side of her outfit, the cardigan would have fallen over her head.

As if on cue, the entire party started to chant. "Chug, chug, chug, chug." She held the position for a good ten seconds before she spit the hose back out. The crowd roared as she was lowed to the floor. "Who's next?" the duo yelled.

"What are they doing?" asked Sarah to Nigel.

"It's called a keg stand. The whole point is to get you drunker quicker. You want to give it a whirl?"

"No," she said shaking her head.

"Here, everyone." Ralph said, holding six shot glasses filled with a clear liquid. He passed two to Nigel and Paul, but the girls rejected the small glasses. "Ladies, come on, we are all friends here. Let's have some fun. It's not like we are getting naked again."

Embarrassed, Sarah looked over to Abby who also turned beet red, likely from previously unpublicized time with Ralph. Hiding their discomfort, each raised a glass for a toast before tipping the rims against their mouths.

As Sarah turned the glass to her lips and the liquor began to flow down her throat, the intense burn set her insides on fire. To extinguish the scorching sensation, she chugged the remainder of the first bottle in her left hand. Still feeling the unsavoriness, she looked toward the fridge, "I need something else to drink."

Nigel handed her another bottle from the fridge. Again, she drank the second one much like a soft drink on a hot summer day. Not ideal, but given it was the first thing she landed her hands on, the quencher worked.

In another corner of the room stood a long table with two triangular alignments of cups. Nigel pointed over as Sarah tossed the empty bottle. "Anyone up for a game of pong? We can play for shirts."

"Not this time," said Emily.

"Alright; we can just play, but girls versus guys for real," said Nigel.

"Emm, I don't need to drink anymore," whispered Sarah.

"I'll drink yours; I just need a partner to play," she replied.

Agreeing to play for Emily's sake, Sarah joined her at the end of the table. The girls initiated the game by hitting both of their targets. Nigel and Paul retaliated in the second round, sinking the same cup. "That makes three," reminded Nigel.

"Sarah, you can drink at least one of these if I drink two." Unwillingly, Sarah did as Emily suggested.

On the following turn, the guys landed two different cups. As Emily reached for both, Nigel asserted that Sarah drink one.

"She can let Emily take them," Paul defended.

"Yeah, but if she doesn't drink her own, she's more likely to hit her shots." Sarah sneered at him. Angry about his suggestion that she was a cheater, she pulled a cup from Emily's hand. Finishing the rest, Sarah slammed the plastic on the table.

Paul and Nigel continued to gain ground as Sarah and Emily began slipping behind. Ultimately, Paul secured the win by sinking the last cup. A visible buzz now captured the party as the music continued to pour through the halls with the drinks following suit.

"Ring of Fire is up next!" yelled a random voice. Everyone cleared the middle of the floor and formed a jagged circle with a can and deck of cards placed in the center. As someone explained the rules, Sarah looked over to Emily. "I think it is time to head back."

"Yeah, me too," Emily said.

"Nonsense," said Ralph as he looped his arms around their shoulders. "You will love this game. It is not much drinking with this many people but still fun to watch and play along."

Sarah tuned to Abby. "Do you need to get back?"

"I am alright now. Ralph said he would walk me home after this game."

Sarah and Emily situated themselves on the opposite side of the guy explaining the game, while Abby clung to Ralph. A strange face appeared, pushing his way in between Emily and Sarah, shifting them over to accommodate. Emily protested that he move, but Sarah assured her it was fine.

Slowly, the group traded off drawing cards as the progression inched closer to them. When a blonde guy three spots to Sarah's right flipped over a Jack, a moan went out. "Never have I," he said. He glanced about the crowd, inspecting faces in a quest for the perfect inquiry. "Alright. Never have I gotten caught fooling around."

Everyone lowered a finger except five lone rangers. Aside from the guy holding the card, there was Emily, Sarah, Abby, and Paul. Nigel retracted a finger while he high-fived the guy next to him. Sarah had always been proud of her conservative approach to life until that moment, as the isolation sunk through her skin. Luckily, the next round the circle of cards was broken, bringing the game to a conclusion.

As Sarah braced on the couch and turned toward the bathroom, Nigel caught her on the shoulder. "Sarah, you don't look like you are having a good time," stammered Nigel. "Try this. It is my own creation.

All the girls love it." Sarah wavered with the idea ever since she had agreed to come to Nigel's party. However, her affection toward Nigel had grown.

Sarah had stepped out of her apartment to find Nigel straddling his Suzuki. "Hop on!" he called. Sarah paused glancing down at her dress. She had not expected him to pick her up on his bike. Masking her shyness, she excused herself and went back inside to quickly slip into a pair of jeans.

"Sorry," she said as she reappeared wearing jeans and a jacket. "I thought we might be walking to the restaurant."

"Ha, jump on." Sarah placed a hand on Nigel's shoulder to disperse the weight as she stepped on the foot peg.

Upon being dropped off that night, Sarah retraced the date in her head. Nigel had been a somewhat unorthodox, but nonetheless a gentleman. He had come to pick her up, took the liberty of paying the bill, and even complemented her beauty. Her insides had fluttered with deep anxiety about their first kiss, much as a puppy would feel when being introduced to its new adopting family: acceptance, affection, and joy.

The two walked side by side to the stoop of Sarah's apartment. "I had a great time tonight," offered Sarah.

"Yeah, me too. You're a really cool girl." Sarah leaned in, opening her arms to hug him goodnight. Almost instantaneously, Nigel interrupted the moment by placing his finger against her lips in a hushing motion. Confused, Sarah stopped and looked long into his eyes. His smile and laugh broke her concentration enough for him to clench her waist, pull Sarah into his body and beckon her to his delectable lips. Unsure of how to react, she followed his lead. Tilting her head back to see Nigel, he met her lips with a slight peck. The kiss was drawn into another and then with a lite bite on her bottom lip. Sarah closed her eyes and allowed Nigel to continue. A tingling sensation trickled gradually over her. Moisture gathered upon the outside of her lips as the tip of his tongue knocked at her closed lips. *What should I do?* If she pulled away, she feared ruining the moment by denying him. Worried about the probability of forfeiting the chance of another date, she parted her lips and allowed his tongue passage.

Their tongues met briefly, before he pulled away. "Well, goodnight," he called, spinning around calmly toward his car. Sarah waved her goodbye over the roar of the motor before she pulled the apartment key from her pocket.

"Sarah, come on, just try this once." His words pulled her back to the party and away from the memory of their date. Choosing to not risk pushing Nigel away, she accepted the cup. The two sat perched on the couch while she sipped on the concoction. "What do you think?"

"It has a berry taste to it; not bad." Sarah checked her watch; it was already a quarter past eleven. "We need to be going," she said to Nigel, glancing around for Emily to no avail.

"Who is we?" he replied.

"Emily. Where did she go?"

"I am not sure, maybe check the bathroom," Nigel replied.

Standing abruptly, all previous balance eluded her. Carefully, Sarah walked the walls back to the kitchen, placing her drink on the bar. Still clinging to the edge of the hallway, she wandered to the bathroom.

Sarah knocked on the door, "Emily, are you in there?" No reply. At first turn, the door refused to click open, but then popped as if the lock had been partially fastened on the other side. Something shoved against the base detoured her from opening the door further than a few inches. Through the crack, she could distinguish two occupants. One was indeed Emily, and the other was the bare back of a recognizable figure, Paul....

Shutting the door, Sarah slumped down against the wall to the floor. *Emily and Paul? Why would they be making out and in a bathroom of all places?*

"What's wrong? Too much to drink for Emily?" asked Nigel.

"Uh yeah, I guess."

"Are you going to check on her?"

"Oh, it's okay. She said she is fine," she lied.

"Is there another bathroom?" asked Sarah.

"Yeah, let me help you up and I'll show ya." Taking her hand, he lifted Sarah off the floor. Together, they cut through the laundry room, to the back staircase that led upstairs. The climb tugged at their legs, causing them to fall forward before reaching the top, yet her thoughts still lagged below.

"You can use the one in my room," he offered, pointing to the door at the far end. "Third door on the left. I share one with a roommate, so just close the door to his side." Sarah followed his instructions down the hall, closing and locking both bathroom doors.

Inside, dirty clothes adorned the corner from an overflowing laundry basket. The shower floor oozed a pinkish black from lack of cleaning. Even with a dark ring lining the bowl, the toilet seat was clean enough to sit on.

After pulling her pants back up, Sarah washed her hands with the little remnants of soap from the dispenser. With the last of the water in her hands, she splashed her face before turning the faucet handle off. Reaching for the sole clean hand towel, she blotted her face dry. Gazing into the mirror at her disheveled appearance, Sarah blinked a few times after noticing her clammy white hands on the counter.

It had been the previous autumn. The patting sound of their shoes on the gravel glided off into the distance of the well-beaten trail. The two had been unable to complete their Sunday long run with the team earlier in the day. Late into the workout, only a glimmer of the sun's rays still shone over the peaks of the nearby mountains.

In the world of cross-country, the long run is where teammates become the closest of friends. A runner's deepest secrets tend to arise as a bond between aloft souls forms, allowing conversations to flow easily from the heart.

After trying to keep an awkward discussion alive the past eight miles, they had covered everything from high school PRs to college majors. Paul was about to give up on his vain efforts, but then the topic transitioned toward future aspirations.

"So, what do you want to do after college?" asked Paul.

"Ha! Well, I would like to get married and maybe start a family," replied Sarah.

"Oh, really? That's great." But before he had realized his next words, he blurted, "What do you look for in a husband?" Caught somewhat off guard, Sarah still did not want to miss the chance of breaking away from the miles spent in silence.

"I guess there are a bunch of characteristics that I look for. You know: kind, gentle, loving…."

"Yeah, that's what most girls say, but what do you really want?" Paul insisted.

Sarah sighed deeply before she continued. "Okay. I can trust you right?"

"Of course," Paul replied.

"There is something that I have always wanted in a man that seems unrealistic… I really want someone that has the same experience as me," she said.

"Experience? What do you mean?"

"I want a guy that hasn't been with any woman except for me."

"Oh." There was a long pause as they rounded the curve and began to climb the sloping path.

Paul rekindled the conversation once topping the hill. "I guess now that you've told me that, I really should tell you one of my secrets."

"Ha. That seems fair enough."

"Well, you see, Sarah, in pure confidence; I have never been with a girl."

That was the moment she first felt drawn toward Paul. That was the moment she would remember forever as the first intimate conversation between them.

The pair traveled down the path for a few more miles as the sun sunk below the horizon, leaving the two with only the guiding light of the moon.

She had lost hope in humanity until that point. Yet that very night she found those hopes being smashed to pieces along with her trust in Paul as she had looked upon him and Emily.

As Sarah returned to his bedroom, Nigel looped his arms around her while embracing in a soft kiss. His adoring presence brought her assurance, warmth, and refuge. He pressed his lips to hers, followed by his tongue. As the heat of the moment rose, the image of Emily and Paul lingered. Making their way to the side of the bed, still locked together, Sarah fell, landing beside Nigel. He gripped her waist and pulled her on top. His hands caressed her thighs and then gently slid back to her waist. Then Nigel sat up and raised his arms to remove his shirt. He paused, looking into Sarah's eyes, waiting.

She hesitated while contemplating his gesture. Nigel had already seen her naked, which she found comfort in knowing, but was she ready to take the relationship further? Leaning up to give her a kiss, Sarah met Nigel halfway but then pushed against his chest with her hand. Sitting back on her heels, she rolled the hair tie over her wrist, fastening her hair into a ponytail.

With a deep breath, Sarah took the bottom hem of her shirt and slid the blouse over her head. Her heavy brown eyes looked down at Nigel, ready for him to secure her in his arms once again.

Nigel gave a slight smile and kissed her on the neck as he reached around to unhook her bra. Tossing the garment, letting it fall to the ground, he smirked. "It's like the beach." Sarah paid no attention to his attempt to ease her thoughts. She merely followed his advance of unbuttoning his jeans by rolling off him and shimmying out of her own. Nigel lay beside her now sweating, bare body, nibbling on her shoulders.

"One sec." Sarah braced up on her elbows, watching as he blindly reached for the nightstand. She fell back on the pillow, falling continuously, never feeling the mattress catch her below.

CHAPTER 14:

A Long Walk

I mages from the night before kept flashing in her head. First, the sight of Emily and Paul, alone in the bathroom, engrossed in each other. Then, the images of her and Nigel shedding their clothes. That was all she could remember, but it was enough to constantly churn at her insides.

The walk back to her apartment stretched down the dark street past various houses, and then a quarter of a mile down a dusty, beaten sidewalk. The sound of thunder had caused her to open her eyes that morning. She was lying beside Nigel in bed. Lifting the covers, she saw they were still naked. Easing out of the blankets, she snuck to the door to the sound of Nigel snoring. As she stooped over for her clothes, she felt a sharp pain in her lower abdomen.

She carried on dressing, nonetheless, memories of last night flooding her mind. She had stopped him for a moment, unsure at first if she was ready. All she knew then was that she did not want to think about Paul and Emily tangled on the bathroom floor.

When Sarah finally made it back to her apartment, her hands quivered as she fumbled with the keys. The absence of a lone light left on for her confirmed that Emily had not returned. She crawled up the stairs to her room and closed the door behind her. Slumping back against the frame, she closed her eyes and took in a deep breath. She wanted to feel fresh, clean, and pure again. Shedding all her clothes and tossing them in the laundry pile, she pulled a towel from the closet. Cold water spewed from the showerhead, stinging her skin until traces of warmer water ascended the pipes.

The blast of steaming water ran like a river down the sides and clefts of her body. Sarah shook with a loneliness she had never experienced before. She again closed her eyes trying to escape the regrets of the previous night, but the scalding water pelted her body awake. The lids of her eyes lifted as a steady flow of tears began to stream down her blush checks. A deep sob emerged as she realized she had hit a breaking point and the pent-up emotions poured out.

Everything hurt, from her stomach to the very walls of her insides. She slumped down to the floor of the bathtub and curled into a ball, arms anchored around her legs. Her head sank until her forehead came to rest on her knees. From the brief flashes she remembered from the previous night, she couldn't recall the actual sex part. She had thought she was ready, but now Sarah was ashamed to consider she allowed herself to venture that far. Still she pondered. Her mind said she would remember something so drastic, but her aching body belied that belief. She had never fathomed it would be like this or hurt so much. The cramps and soreness were nearly unbearable.

Last semester, she had overheard a few girls discussing their first times, complaining about the pain. However, they hadn't mentioned the immensity of the pain, only that they stopped because the discomfort was concerning.

What have I done? She no longer considered herself a sweet, innocent girl. She failed to stop as she should have and allowed her emotions to take control.

After loathing in the bottom of the shower, Sarah found it within herself to finish bathing. Once she turned the water off, she pulled the towel around her chest and stepped out. Some comfort resided in washing away the dried sweat and stench from the evening; however, only when she was dressed in clean clothes and no longer naked did the grungy, gross feeling depart. Sarah plopped down hard onto her mattress. She hoped she could sleep this off, hoped that when she woke up it would all be a terrible dream. She hoped, but the desired sleep tarried, hopeless to clear her mind.

An unsettling question brought more worry. Was Nigel wearing protection? After experiencing a frantic episode during a lab, her latex allergy required the use of special gloves to prevent her hands from breaking out. However, no apparent rashes had formed, or irritation could be seen in the shower, only soreness. *What if I get a pregnancy test? What if I just ask Nigel what had happened? Or would that freak him out? Both of those are too embarrassing, and birth control ... I couldn't. No, it would be better to wait first and see if I'm ... pregnant. My period should start in just under a week.* If she was pregnant, then telling her parents, and ... and Nigel would be unavoidable. *Oh, Nigel! How will I handle it the next time I see him? What would he say?* The tears began to pour again as she thought of what the future might hold. Whether from the exhaustion of worrying or from the lack of sleep, the tears finally ceased, and she faded off to sleep.

Heartbreak surrounded Sarah the remainder of the weekend and into Monday. When Emily questioned her whereabouts, Sarah fought through the urge to confide in Emily, convincing her she merely left the party and walked home. Emily confessed her trip to the bathroom after the games ended was caused by nausea, not mentioning Paul. Whether her claim of composing herself and passing out on the couch was true was debatable. So on Sunday, Sarah chose to run solo, struggling to complete the twelve-mile workout while tormented in her own thoughts.

Unsure if she could garner the strength and courage to face anyone else from the party, Sarah decided to skip her classes on Monday. She knew she would be unable to miss practice without raising concern, but a day off from school seemed plausible.

The car hummed over the pavement vibrating the silent air inside. "Everything alright, Sar?"

Sarah considered her front failed to fool Emily. "You must be getting nervous," Emily said.

Nervous? Sarah thought. *Did she hear something about the party? How did she know?* "Nervous?" she asked.

"Yeah … is it because region is a week away?"

"Oh yeah… I am just focused on getting ready for the race."

As they parked at the far end of the row of cars, Sarah gritted her teeth. Paul and Nigel, along with Abby, were standing around listening to Ralph spout off one of his stories. When she got out of the car, Sarah turned toward them to see if anyone was looking her way, but no one noticed.

Even during the stretching, no one mentioned the party or conveyed any indication that gossip had spread. Oddly, Nigel was talking to everyone on the team, carefree, but yet to acknowledge her. Paul and Emily traded hellos without a hint of sexual tension. Through the whole practice, Sarah worried in silence. This was their last grueling workout before regionals, so conversation was sparse.

As Sarah and Emily finished their next-to-last repeat, Nigel readied to start his final rep. Unconsciously, her glance fell his direction, their eyes meeting in a glance. An unsavory lurch tugged at her insides as his gaze penetrated down to her soul. Sarah knew her glossed eyes hung full of pain, the usual beauty they possessed having vanished. Nigel's expression displayed concern, yet as she walked by, he merely smiled.

Her chest throbbed, aching as the dagger thrust into her heart. *He had to remember most of what happened. And it wasn't like he was seeing someone else, or was he?* Sarah tried to shake loose of the cold grasp of denial, but she instead lowered her head. As she stepped up for her last lap, she pressed down, leaving Emily to fall behind and finishing ten seconds ahead of pace.

"Alright, Sarah, I know you are excited, but save it for region," yelled Coach.

With deep breaths, Sarah came to rest along the track, with her hands on her hips. Sliding a hand under her shirt, she worked to pinch a cramping stomach muscle, but the skin remained tight. Forgetting the side stitch, she hunched over at the onset of another abdominal episode. A breathless Emily broke between breaths, "I didn't know … you wanted to race … on that last one."

"I didn't; just getting in a good last effort," Sarah replied.

Sarah looked around, but Nigel was nowhere to be seen. Peering back toward the cars, she noticed him standing by his bike talking to the other guys who had finished their workouts.

Sarah ached to tell Emily everything right then and there, but she couldn't. If she told her about spending the night with Nigel, Emily would know she caught Paul and her in the bathroom, and they both would have to admit lying to the other.

More importantly, Sarah was still hurt at Emily. Emily had known she liked Paul and that failed to stop the two from getting overly cozy. *Who knows if she actually slept on the couch that night or ended up in a bed with Paul?* Insisting on not wanting to revisit the party, Sarah turned and started to walk back to the cars.

Sarah concentrated her stare away from the ground, and her focus anywhere but on Nigel. Unsure if she could handle the truth, she resisted the urge to confront him. Additionally, if she questioned him openly, everyone would hear about their promiscuous moments, which sounded almost as terrifying as an unplanned pregnancy.

As she opened Emily's passenger door, a hand caught her by the arm. It was Nigel. "Hey, Sarah!" She turned around, but her voice eluded her.

"Did you throw up in my bathroom the other night?" *Throw up? He was asking if I threw up in his bathroom?* Nothing about her getting home safe, or missing class, or anything that happened. He was concerned about his bathroom.

"No, I did not."

"Oh, okay, someone must have earlier." Without waiting for a reply, he left.

Sarah stewed in the car waiting for Emily to join her. She wondered whether the frustration stimulated more from his carelessness or the fact he only seemed to care about his bathroom. As she sat in complete disarray, a terrifying flashback rattled her memory. She had visited the bathroom just before they made out, and clearly recalled nothing being particularly clean, but no one had thrown up. *So, if it was clean before-hand, that could only mean ... Someone had wandered in while we were naked.* Her eyes grew in astonishment. *Who was it? More importantly, had they known it was me?*

The driver's side door opened and Emily jumped into the car. "Glad the last hard practice of the season is over," sighed Emily. "We should celebrate."

"Yeah," replied Sarah.

"How about we go out for Mexican?"

"That sounds delicious, Emm."

"Should we invite anyone else?"

Without hesitation, Sarah answered, "No, let's just us go." She was still upset with Emily, but she'd rather be anywhere else then than with the guys.

Dragging herself up the stairs, Sarah shed her clothes as the door shut behind her. She yearned for a shower. The weight of her arms proved challenging as she rinsed her body. The attempt to raise her hands and wash her hair was the only excuse she needed to forgo shampooing another day. With little more than a spritzing off, Sarah pulled back the shower curtain, blindly reaching for a towel.

Droplets of water splashed the floor as she padded her face dry. Wrapping the towel over her shoulders, she only considered drying off before moving to her waist, eventually dropping the towel at her feet. Still damp, she collapsed on her mattress with only her bare skin pressed to the sheets. Leaning back, she shut her eyes for a few moments.

A knock at the door, followed by Emily's appearance over her face, hardly disturbed Sarah. "What are you doing, Sar? Get dressed."

"I just needed a nap. Can you help me up?" Sarah asked.

"Coach told you not to go all out at practice," said Emily as she reached to pull Sarah from her bed. Sarah's skin now laden with chill bumps nudged her to find clothes.

"What are you wearing to eat, Emm?"

"I may just put on sweats."

"I like that idea," said Sarah.

Emily pulled a set from Sarah's closet and tossed them to her before undoubtedly going to change herself. Emily's overlook of underwear provoked the instinct to call out, but Sarah instead donned the sweats without them, forgoing Emm's servitude.

"Should we drive or walk? How about we walk?" said Emily upon her return.

"I am not really feeling up to walking," said Sarah.

"You probably just need something to eat, and the restaurant is just around the corner." Emily tucked the keys back into her purse, motioning Sarah to follow.

The array of empty chairs seemed abnormal, even for a Monday. Aside from an older man, they were the only diners.

"Have a seat wherever you like," said a waiter. Sarah walked toward a nook hidden along the far side. A greasy guy who appeared less than enthused to be working, meandered from the kitchen to take their order. "What do you want?"

Sarah, half-serious and half-annoyed, answered, "How about a drink?"

"We have half-price margaritas right now."

"Make that two," said Emily.

When the waiter returned, he produced two additional smaller glasses. "Complimentary shots on the house, since we're slow."

Emily stuck her nose to the rim. "Tequila," she said as the two emptied the shots into their bigger glasses before stirring them together with a straw.

As they slurped from their glasses, the waiter circled back for their orders. "Okay, one enchilada, and one burrito. Do you need a refill while I am here?" He lifted a pitcher of margaritas from the adjacent table, undisturbed since he first served them.

"Sure," said Sarah.

By the time the plates were placed in front of them, the girls were on their third glass, manifesting in an impaired state on an empty stomach. The two began to joke and laugh as if neither withheld any secrets from the other. Sarah no longer thought about Paul, and the worries of pregnancy had vanished.

Not until they abandoned the stability of the table did Sarah take notice of herself. Both stammered their words and moved in an uncontrollable gait. At one point, they fell to the ground, merely laughing at the dubious effort to stand up.

Stumbling inside the apartment, Emily and Sarah trudged up the stairs before collapsing on their beds. As Sarah looked at the ceiling, her head began spinning with the stationary fan. Quickly, the whimsical mood was replaced with fear. She needed to get up, and fast. Sarah rolled over the side of the bed and onto the floor. Gathering what strength and focus she could, she crawled along the carpet and linoleum. Barely hinging her head over the toilet, Sarah relinquished everything from dinner.

With the contents of her stomach emptied, Sarah retreated from the bowl with bits clumped in her hair. A streak of bile stained the sleeve she used to wipe her mouth. Her vision drifted in and out while she curled in a ball on the bathroom floor.

Knotted stomach muscles tensed like a wet washcloth being wrung dry. She looked around, but there was no sign that Emily had flocked to her side at the sound of distress. She must have gone to sleep. Sarah grasped the side of the sink, pulling herself to her knees. Peering up, she saw a flushed, disheveled girl looking back at her. Momentarily, Sarah worried she was not alone, for the unfamiliar woman who appeared in the mirror could not have been her.

With a migraine and shredded stomach, Sarah set out the next day to begin the weeklong taper leading to the pivotal race. As she approached a clearing on the trail, she sauntered over to the path's edge that towered above the town.

Sitting atop the rock overlooking the vast valley below, Sarah could not help but feel small. The soft wind grew still at the face of the mountain, while the autumn sun glowed on her skin. Trying to let it all go, even for just a minute, seemed impossible. If only she could move away from the past. Night terrors, self-loathing, and subtle reminders kept popping up. She wanted to be alone, but she also wished someone were there to provide comfort. She lay back against the ground and opened her eyes to the sky. Above a few clouds and a small bird hovered. The bird circled her body imitating a vulture closing in on an afternoon meal. *Is that all I am now, just a rotting piece of flesh not fit for anything? Why? Why did this happen to me?* Her whole life she tried to do the right thing, but in one night, all that work and effort seemed to be undone.

CHAPTER 15:

Region

A rriving in the middle of the night and settling into their hotel rooms, the team was summoned outside for a twenty-minute walk.

"Loosen your legs up and then straight to bed," Coach said.

The guys circled the hotel in one direction as the girls headed in the other. The length of the hotel called for two laps around the perimeter. Both instances that Sarah passed Nigel, she quickly feigned interest in the other girls' conversation, only to revert to herself as the guys moved out of sight.

A rickety elevator vibrated as the pulleys churned between floors. The abrupt landing on the seventh floor interrupted Sarah's yawn. Her nerves had eased with the departure of the guys, two floors earlier. Sarah headed straight to the queen-sized bed, forgoing washing up, dozing off briefly to the sound of Emily running the shower; constant tossing impeded a sound rest throughout the night.

With certainty, Sarah managed four hours of intermittent sleep. When the alarm relayed its beckon, she already lay awake anticipating a break in the endless tussle.

Countless highs and one devastating low had led her to this moment, the morning of region. The natural butterflies in her stomach were replaced by a cringing sensation as cramps became unpredictable. Sweat clouded Sarah's hands as she hopelessly went to the bathroom. She was five days late.

Given any circumstances, this race would rank as the most important she ever ran, but today it would also prove the toughest. The thoughts that she was mentally and physically prepared were rattled by the hands of life. She had always heard that whatever physical routine a woman followed before pregnancy, she could safely continue after conception. So, if she was pregnant, she needn't worry about causing any issues. At least, that was her thought process. She had to focus, so her thoughts could ride solely on the chance to reach the pinnacle of her running career.

"Are you going down for breakfast with the team, Sar?"

"Not today; I want to try and get my mind ready for the race," she replied.

"Alright, I will meet you at the bus then. I want to go ahead and eat so I'll load my bag now." Then turning toward the door, Emily headed into the hallway, leaving Sarah behind.

She was nervous at this point. The cramps had subsided for now, allowing her to focus on the task at hand. Sarah combed through her bag once more to make sure she was not leaving anything. At the bottom of her gym bag lay a hair tie. As her fingers touched the band, images of her and Nigel flashed in her mind, images filled with disbelief. She tossed the tie back to the bottom, concealing the affliction with a towel and her spikes.

Frantically, she searched for a substitute to fasten her hair for the race. Folding back the partially unzipped side pocket, she fumbled inside. Entangled with strains of hair lay what she had hoped to find, hair clips. Wrapping her hair into a bun, she sighed in relief. Sarah completed a last inspection of the room, and then grabbed her bag and a water bottle from the nightstand before awaiting an empty elevator.

The sliding doors opened to Coach standing near the entrance peeling an orange. "Are you ready, kiddo? No pressure, but the rankings came out yesterday."

"You are seeded third and Emily is seventh." Sarah nodded at the news.

"Third, huh?"

"Yeah, doesn't that just rub you raw? Now get on the bus and you go show them you didn't come here to be less than the best." Sarah hated losing, but she despised more being overlooked before a race even started.

Staring down at the ground, still considering coach's words, she made her way outside following the glow of the bus. For such an occasion, the team was allowed a roomy coach bus with enough space for everyone to sit by themselves. Sarah picked a seat halfway back in the row behind Emily's bag. She stared out of the window, but the darkness outside left the glass casting a faint reflection of her. This would be her day, and she had no intention of letting anything stand in her way.

It was as if the bus doors reopened just as the team had gotten settled in their seats. "Everybody up," yelled Coach. "Girls you are first, followed by the guys' race about fifty minutes later."

Duffle bags bounced between seats as they unloaded in silence. There were no jokes made, no small talk heard. Each had trained and planned the six months since untying their track spikes at the conclusion of the outdoor season. Jumping from the bottom step off the bus, they were met with cold, dry air. Coach provided clear instructions, "You must be sweating before you get on the line, or you will not be starting." This would be a challenge with today's temperatures. All of the runners jogged their warmups, layered in sweats, tights, and whatever else they found. However, the weather would be in the high 40s by eight o'clock, meaning Sarah would continue as usual, without her tights during the race.

Coach Cavlere and a freshman carried the tent to the sole remaining opening wide enough to accommodate the tarp. If this were any other race, the top guys would have overseen the fortification of their settlement. Once the tarp's corners were flattened, Sarah and Emily dropped their gear before commencing to warm up. Still in silence, they followed the course banners, acquainting their legs with the layout.

The circuit's hills forced sweat to bead on her brow first, and then in the crevices of her body, but not enough to cause a chill from the dampness. Passing the loop indicator, the group veered off toward the finish chute. Sarah envisioned racing down the final stretch as the pandemonium reached a climax. She felt ready.

An announcement crackled over the loudspeakers placed around the staging area, declaring the ten-minute warning until the start of the women's race. After switching into her spikes, Sarah began stripping off her sweats. All that remained was her formfitting forest green sleeveless jersey and her black race shorts. Her thin legs and arms offered no fat as protection from the breeze. Goosebumps crawled down her extremities as she tossed the layers into her bag. A second call echoed over the field, "All ladies to the line."

Sarah and Emily stood side to side as they readied to toe the line. The wind died down as a calm hush fell over the crowd. The announcer buzzed over the speakers. "There will be a two command start, I will say on your mark, and then when everyone is set, I will fire the gun." Sarah shook out her legs one last time.

"On your mark." Pow! The stampede of girls exploded from the line, shaking the earth and nearby spectators. The field stretched three hundred meters before corralling into the roped-off section. Sarah knew she must break to the front or lose precious time.

As they neared the shift, Sarah and Emily managed to separate from the pack, landing themselves within the top twenty competitors. It was always a relief to release the constrained energy and nerves from the start and settle into her given race pace. Sarah's goal was simple: run 5:35 for each mile, making sure to either stay at pace and leave the other girls, or adjust to keep with the head pack to force a sprint off at the end. No matter which, Sarah knew the fight for first would prove tough. The other girls sought the same success, but none would prosper without a limitless effort.

As they approached the first mile, Sarah fell into her rhythm. Three girls stayed ahead of her, but only by a second or two. With an over-the-shoulder glance, she could see Emily following close behind. A free-standing clock and a cheering crowd greeted them as they passed the mile marker. 5:31, 5:32, 5:33, 5:34, 5:35 … Coach Cavlere's voice carried over the rumble of shouting, "Stay with them Sarah and Emily, push each other."

Veering from the crowd, the course turned left to loop back around. A few of the girls bumped into each other, tension growing in angst not to trip over one another. A foreign hand slammed into Sarah's shoulder, allowing the girl to brace a fall and remain on her feet. Sarah barely broke stride. Emerging on the other side of the bend, the group's stride quickened, a move noticeable enough to provoke mind tricks without stimulating fatigue. Sarah and Emily hastened their tempo to stay with the other girls. There was plenty of time left to race, but they dared not drop behind.

The next segment consisted of the infamous hill followed by the break toward the finish line on the last lap. As they met at the base, Emily pulled alongside of Sarah, and then advanced toward the front. Without hesitation, Sarah stepped in line, concentrating her stare on the small of Emily's back. By the halfway point, they had passed the lead girl. An immediate descent followed the cresting; Emily and Sarah now ran hip to hip. Coasting the downward slope, they closed in on the halfway mark.

Sarah could hear the other girls' faint whispers of breathing in her ear. Despite obtaining the lead, the lure to win increased the pace. A few girls, including Emily, followed. Sarah couldn't position herself to see behind, but felt a sizable lead growing as she continued running out front. The next corral of spectators assured her thoughts with cheers lagging five seconds between her and the others. *This is it*, she thought. *Just keep going.*

They circled around to where Coach waited, indicating that just over a mile was left in the race. Cavlere whispered to her loud enough to pierce her concentration, but faint enough to escape everyone else's attention. "Don't let them take this from you." The words sent her brain into flight. She peeked over her shoulder to check the others' whereabouts. Charging forward, she feared their footsteps were growing closer. One of the girls caught her, and then slowly inched ahead. *No*, she thought. "You are not taking this from me," she mumbled under her breath. She could hear more footsteps closing in on her. She knew one set belonged to Emily.

Another three quarters of a mile separated them from the finish. Sarah nipped at the heels of the lead girl that stood between her and the regional championship. The half-mile point was when Sarah usually made her move. Her kick was good for eight hundred meters, but the fight to the finish would persist beyond, leaving little margin for the lead. She would have to be prepared at two hundred meters to make her signature move of an overpowering kick. This time for all the marbles.

The course rose as they mounted the last hill. Reaching the top meant a visible finish from a quarter of a mile. A flat final stretch, but no downhill recovery time.

Sarah transitioned to a modified kick as she climbed upward, joining the top girl before ending the dead heat. Three girls comprised the lead group: Sarah: the standout from Cypress University, Natalie Penbar, and then Emily. A rush of adrenaline flooded Sarah's body as she realized the prime positioning. Sarah allowed her body to have control, only aware of the wind sweeping her face and the jumble of the crowd's cry as the three barreled toward the finish. Only three hundred meters left. Emily's stamina diminished as Natalie rejoined Sarah at the hip.

The two streamed through the banner-lined path, steadily increasing the pace. Two hundred meters: *One more push*, Sarah thought. She let the last bit of strength release into her body. There was nothing else to give. Nothing left to borrow from. Only will. The instant Sarah transitioned to her finishing move, Natalie's momentum faltered .... A regional title would be hers. The roar of the crowd intensified into the last one hundred meters. *Just a little further,* she thought. *Just keep pushing... just keep fighting.* The crowd-lined ropes zoomed by in a blur. The sounds grew faint. At fifty meters, Sarah trembled. Something was wrong. Something she never felt before covered her body. The breath escaped from her lungs ... She felt cold, dizzy, darkness, then limp ....

Hushed voices bounced around her head as she regained consciousness. Shaded outlines surrounded her. She fluttered her eyelids a few times, but the sensations proved too intense. Her lifeless body was rolled over and lifted onto a gurney. With the slamming of doors and the ambulance sirens ringing, total darkness was followed by silence.

Days or hours had passed when Sarah finally opened her eyes. Confusion dogged her mind, preventing the recollection of events. She cautiously crooked her neck toward the bedside where a man sat, leg crossed over his knee, with a newspaper folded open. Lowering the paper, the stranger revealed himself as Coach Cavlere. "What happened?"

"You blacked out. Not unusual for distance runners to collapse insight of the finish, but I dare say you did more than collapse. We thought we lost you for a minute."

Sarah lowered her head, reading the hospital ID bracelet loosely draped around her wrist. "What happened after I went down?"

He hesitated for a second. "Well you out kicked Natalie, and Emily was not far behind. Once you left the Cypress girl, she faded hard, and the next thing everyone saw was Emily breaking the finish line tape. I think she even had her eyes closed, because she didn't see you go down. Or at least that's the last I saw as I ran over to you."

"Is anyone else here?"

"No," he replied. "Abby stopped me before I left, but I advised her to head home and tell the others you need to rest. I stayed so you wouldn't be alone and hopefully I can take you back to school once you're released."

As a testament to their friendship, she would have never left Emily's side. She sank into the bed, contemplating such betrayal.

"What's that?" asked Sarah, looking at the ribbon that dangled from her coach's hand. He opened his fingers, revealing a metallic circle tethered to the ribbon. "Abby left this for you. She finished in the top ten but wanted you to have it." Sarah smiled as he laid the medal on the bed sheet.

The bubbling frustration subsided just as the nurse entered the room. "Hi. Sarah. I'm Madeline. Glad to see you are up. Mr. Cavlere, if you can excuse us for a minute, I need to check to make sure everything looks fine. Thank you again, sir, for keeping an eye on her."

Coach nodded and opened the door. "I am going to the cafeteria to get something to eat, but I will be back in about half an hour."

"That will be fine, sir, the doctor will be in before then and will want to talk to Miss Sarah."

"Talk to me about what? What is wrong?"

"Everything is fine; you can relax. Since you were unconscious, we needed to run tests to determine why you passed out. It is strictly protocol to take blood samples first, and then go from there. The doctor will just want to discuss those results."

The nurse took hold of Sarah's left arm, rotating her palm face up. "Just want to make sure the IV is still in place. We put in a drip to stabilize your liquids and help with dehydration. How are you feeling now?"

"Really exhausted, and a little lightheaded," Sarah replied.

"Okay; the doctor should be in any moment. I will let you rest until he comes, and then I will be back." With a warm smile, she turned and left the room. Sarah reclined on the pillow and shut her eyes.

Dr. H. C. Graves knocked with an authoritative rap that resonated in the air. Sarah's heartbeat quickened upon his entrance. In one hand, he carried a folder that appeared to contain her medical reports. The other held a Band Aid. "Here you go, Sarah." He removed the old bandage, then pulled back the wrapper, and neatly laid the cartoon Snoopy bandage over the site of the needle puncture. She gave a small laugh at his act. She had loved the furry canine since she was a toddler and seeing the familiar beagle put her at ease.

"Sarah, I am Doctor Graves. How are you?"

"Just tired and a little lightheaded."

"Have you been feeling fatigued?"

"I guess, but we run so much, it's hard to tell. I've had many restless nights lately, too."

He grimaced, pulling his lips up as if in deep thought and nodded. Opening the folder, he read over the notes, confidently a second time. "Well, Sarah; I am afraid I have some bad news."

Her insides sank, and a blanket of fear cloaked her. "After you arrived, we ran blood tests to determine what happened."

This was it, the news she had been dreading to hear. She was pregnant, and likely her body just fell apart due to the stress. She had thought racing would be fine, but apparently, she was wrong. "Sarah, the findings show that you are indeed, undoubtedly ... anemic."

"I am what?"

"Anemic. It means your blood is lacking the right levels of ferritin for you to function properly. That's why you passed out. Usually with this condition, you lose all of your gusto, sort of speak. You don't have the energy to do normal activities without issues. However, here, your problem escalated. Doing so, your body finally had enough, and was starting to shut down. Hence, the fainting." For a second, she was relieved to hear this news, but the doctor noted the satisfied look on her face. "Something tells me there is a part of the story you're withholding." Sarah frowned like a child being scolded by her parents.

Following a long pause, "There is something... You see, a few weeks ago, a guy I was seeing invited me to a party with some friends. We ended up alone, caught in the moment. I don't remember what all really happened because after our clothes came off, everything is a blur. The next day when I woke up ... we were still naked. I don't remember having sex, but since then my lower abdomen and other areas have been extremely sore. And now I am late for my period," she blurted out.

"Um hummm," said the doctor as he flipped through the pages. "Just how late are you?"

"About a week now, I suppose."

"Well, Sarah, according to the blood tests, the hormone levels in your body were checked as well, and based on the measurements, I would say the chances that you are pregnant are negligible." Sarah slumped back into the bed, overcome with relief. "You see if you were that late, your hormone levels would be elevated. There is a very simple explanation, though. When women compete at high levels, such as you do, it is not uncommon for them to lose their periods. Your body only has enough energy to supply the three major requirements: growth, repair, and reproduction. When you are under high amounts of physical stress, your body needs more energy for repairing and growing new muscles. That leaves nothing for reproduction to steal from."

"So why am I having cramps, and does that mean I can't have kids?"

"No, no. The cramps are likely related to the severe anemia you have, and the cycle will resume itself once you maintain a suitable lifestyle without so much running."

"That's good to hear, but I have one other question doctor."

"Yes?"

"I've been having intense night sweats where I wake up and my sheets are soaked. I thought night sweats were for women going through menopause."

"Well it is, but again your body does strange things under stress. This could be triggered by your running, or if you have been consuming large amounts of alcohol, or a mixture of the two," he said, lifting his eyebrows. "For now, I am going to recommend you lay off the running. You need to give your body time to heal. I would say at least until your regular cycle resumes. Also, you will need to take an iron supplement every day and eat better. That will resolve your anemia. Otherwise, you should be fine. I'm going to release you to go home, so once your discharge papers are filed, you will be free to go."

"Thank you, doctor."

He gave a soft smile, "Take care."

CHAPTER 16:

Fallout

The silver truck shifted to park as Coach dropped her off at the front door, "Thanks again, Coach, for looking after me. And for the cab ride back to campus."

"Anytime, kiddo; now go get some rest."

Her shoulders slumped to ease the tension from her muscles. Fortunately, her season was over. Additionally, the girls had failed to capture enough points, and the guys' performance lacked the dominance for national berths. Sarah knew Cavlere's frustration toward their performance was only displaced by his concern for her. The thought of hibernating throughout winter appealed to her mind as she shut the truck door in disappointment.

Inside, the apartment was silent. She was alone. Obeying her Coach's advice, Sarah clung to the handrail as she slinked up the stairs.

The bubbling of voices outside perked her ears open. Sarah pulled back the covers to investigate from the window. Emily and Paul walked along the sidewalk, wrapped in each other's arms as they approached the front door. Emily reared her head and snorted as Paul attempted to tickle her. The laughter faded as she noticed Sarah at the window. Retreating out of sight, Sarah twisted the lock on her bedroom door.

Emily's goodbye to Paul ended shortly after, for soon she made her presence known with a soft knock. "Hey, Sarah. Are you okay? I am so sorry about what happened. Do you want to talk?"

"No, you should just be worried about yourself … and Paul."

"Sarah, let me in. Are you mad about me winning, or about Paul and me? Or both?" Sarah buried her face in her pillow to muffle any response. "I didn't see you at the finish, honest. And Coach didn't want us visiting the hospital. And Paul and I, well we just kind of grew together." Sarah's silence resonated out into the hall. "Fine, be mad," shouted Emily as she stormed off to her room.

The rest of the week, silence stood between them. Sarah remained a hostage to her room, only leaving for class or an unaccompanied meal, confiding in no one. By Friday afternoon, Thanksgiving break was upon them as everyone packed to return home.

Following a few hours on the interstate and twisting side roads to her hometown, Sarah pulled into her parents' driveway at 733 Timber Way. The brick structure was a simple house built just before she was born. The Mills were high school sweethearts whose history entailed no other romances. This was the kind of relationship Sarah always hoped for, yet it still eluded her.

While the family dog, Daisy, waited eagerly on the porch, her brother wasn't so reserved. Matty, twelve years her junior, mimicked every move she made in admiration. With her commitments to cross-country and the trip to the beach, he had missed seeing her all semester. Racing out the door, he jumped and tugged at her arms in expectation of a hug.

Daisy stayed on the floor patiently waiting her turn to be acknowledged. Once Matty loosened his clinch, Sarah smiled and leaned over to scratch Daisy's stomach.

"Mom's in the kitchen making chili for dinner, and dad is on his way home from work," Matty said, speeding off to proclaim Sarah's arrival. Her mom, emptying her ladle, dropped her apron on the counter before reaching out to Sarah.

"Hey, Liv. I am so glad your home. Matty, help Sarah Olivia take those bags upstairs. Dinner will be ready in about twenty minutes."

Snatching the luggage, Matty jetted up the stairs, disappearing before Sarah could offer a helping hand.

With steaming bowls of chili poured and a cobbler centered on the table, Sarah's dad asked the blessing. She struggled to remember the last time she had prayed. During the past month of tribulations, it was disheartening to realize that she had forgotten. Lifting their heads, Cliff passed a sleeve of crackers to Sarah before asking, "So, what is new? How did the race go?"

A practiced story filtered through her head, as she sipped on a glass of water. "Well, I did not win, but I did PR. Those girls were definitely good and gave me a run for my money."

"Who won?" asked Matty. Considering the distance between the Mills and Ellis families and the slim media coverage of a regional cross-country title, Sarah easily could have fibbed. However, Sarah met his innocent eyes and could not lie to her little brother.

"Actually, it was my friend Emily."

"Oh, Liv, I know that must have been a tough break."

"Thanks, Mom. It was hard, but it just was not my day. I gave it everything I could though."

"You must have placed pretty well then because you and Emily are pretty close in speed, right?"

"Well, yeah, but she was with the lead pack, and I fell back a little by the end. I got a side stitch, and it threw off my race. I ended up in the top ten, which is alright."

"That's great, Sarah. We are so proud of you."

"Can I see your medal?" asked Matty. In keeping a tight alibi, Sarah had almost forgotten about Abby's gift.

"Yeah, sure, I have it in my backpack," she remembered.

Seeing his intrigued expression, Sarah's pride dissolved with the crackers in her soup. Telling them a fabricated version left an icky after-taste. However, she couldn't tell the truth. If she brought up her anemia, she feared their questions would lead to the hospital and eventually Nigel. She could only imagine bringing up something as censored as sex. Then disappointment would poke its ugly head, only making the situation worse.

Scrapping the bowl for a final bite, she muffled a small burp. Excusing herself from the table, she went upstairs to shower before turning down the bed.

Still unsnapping the last few blouse buttons, Sarah paused at the sound of a knock. "Hey, Sarah, is everything going okay? I know you must be upset about Emily winning, but you did not seem yourself tonight."

"Yeah, I am fine. It was just a tough season, and not really what I hoped would happen for an outcome." Not willing to push the subject, her mom gave her a hug and a kiss on the forehead.

"Well, if you need to talk, just let me know. Don't worry about Emily. It's not the end of the world because your friend upset you. Sometimes, we must settle on being happy for them, and in return, you'll usually find peace with the matter. Also, I think you're forgetting, there's a whole track season ahead. If you only had a cramp, Emily better be on her toes come this spring."

Sarah smiled, "Thanks, Mom. You always know how to make me feel better."

After their discussion, the week's progression brought more clutter to the kitchen and less of the muddle from the past few months lodged in the back of her mind. Thursday morning centered around the television, watching the Thanksgiving Day Parade. This year, Cliff and Megan played hosts for the Thanksgiving dinner. Sarah's grandparents, aunts, uncles, and even a new baby cousin stuffed the living and dining rooms. Megan, with Sarah's assistance, exceeded previous traditional feasts by preparing every imaginable fixing to serve with the turkey. While Sarah busied herself creating the dishes she knew, Matty and Cliff manned the smoker, keeping an eye on the turkey.

Fine china appeared only twice a year at the Mills' house, during Thanksgiving and Christmas. The plates showed clear signs of aging, some marked with nicks from use. Sarah pulled a step stool to the counter to help reach the plates on the top shelf. Seeing Sarah stretch for another set, Megan fished a stack of paper throwaways from the cabinets.

"I got these for the kids to use." Sarah knew her mom treasured the sentiment of the china, handed down from Sarah's great grandmother as a wedding gift to her parents. Aside from the bend of the loaded paper, no one would be the wiser.

Matty was the last to discard his plate, only stopping after scraping the last bite from the pan of cornbread dressing. He settled next to Sarah in front of the television to watch the lighting of the Macy's Christmas tree. Sarah had missed her family. With them, life proved much simpler and relaxing. *Maybe more relaxing for some than others*, she thought gleefully as her uncle's snore drew attention from her own fatigue.

Megan's niece stirring disbanded the close circle as Sarah's aunt and uncle headed home. One by one, they bid relatives goodnight through early evening.

"I think it is your bedtime, Matty," Megan announced.

"But, Mom, Sarah is here and it's not a school night." She looked through Matty to Sarah, who consented to his plea with a nod.

"Alright then, but not past eleven. I don't want to have to drag you out of bed tomorrow morning." The extension granted Matty a few additional hours, but the request went unneeded.

Matty lay sprawled over Sarah's bed, admiring the medal pulled from her bag. Yawning, he murmured, "I hope I can be as fast as you some day."

"You will be faster, Matty."

"How do you know?"

"Trust me," she said.

He examined the piece until his grasped loosened at the onset of sleep.

Sarah threaded her arms beneath him, but as she attempted to lift his body, Matty wrestled away only to walk himself to his own bed. With everyone asleep, Sarah sat against the headboard looking around her old room. The time capsule bore a collection of eighteen years' worth of memories. Reminiscing gave her a moment of serenity before pressing a hand against the medal pulled forth the unpleasant recent memories.

Sarah knelt beside her bed to say her prayers for the night. She spoke the words, but no sensation accompanied the petition. Conceding to the fruitless labor, she crawled from the floor and into bed. Tears speckled her quivering checks.

A few short months ago, life was graced with hope and promise. Now, her faith had diminished, dissolving a once coveted self-trust. *It is impossible to believe in God when I don't believe in myself.* It had been a while since she could say she believed in anything. The lingering thought and strain of tears lulled her to sleep.

No nearby streetlights or passing cars interrupted the night, but Sarah was woken by a deep throbbing inside her. She scurried from the covers and ran to the bathroom. Blindly searching for the toilet seat, half-asleep and half-conscious, she realized the source of her disturbed slumber. What once evaded her had now returned. Sarah always dreaded starting her cycle until that night. Carefully, she shuffled to search for a tampon. A bin tucked in the vanity cabinet between towels and toilet paper held only an empty box. Hopes of a spare reverted Sarah to her purse. Digging blindly through her bag brought no luck. In desperation, she reached to the bottom, giving a sigh of relief as her fingers landed on the cylindrical wrapper. As she removed her hand, a thick and misplaced object caught her attention.

Lying in the corner of the pink purse rested a folded piece of paper. The notebook paper had been folded neatly many times so it would fit in that very corner. Puzzled to what she stumbled upon, she opened the top of the purse wide enough to peer down to the bottom. The white, blue lined, sheet molded in a small square stood out amongst the other occupants. Still grasping the tampon, she tiptoed back to the bathroom before returning to the unexpected mystery.

The hesitation to peel the folded edges back was overcome by curiosity. Straightening the first crease of the parcel revealed five single letters. Written with an underlined slash below read the name:

Sarah

She almost began to cry as she held the letter between her fingers. So simple. So personal. The handwriting was all too familiar; no further inspection would have been necessary for a sender, but she knew reading the contents was a must.

As she traversed the lines that covered the page, she read slowly as to take in every word like a deep breath. Not knowing what the next words might proclaim, she read eagerly to the end. Sarah gripped the paper tightly as she continued down the page, growing more nervous the further she read. Upon reaching the bottom and seeing the name, she began to cry.

Sarah,

I have been thinking a lot lately. What I am going to do after college, how will cross-country go this year, and what do I want out of life? Over the past year, we have become better friends and I want to take that to the next level. The problem is, I do not know if that is what you're looking for. You fit every aspect that I want in a girlfriend, and I know we have very similar stances in life that we cherish. I must be honest though. If you want to be in a relationship, then I am already there. However, if you don't, then I just need to know. Either way, we can still be friends, but I don't want to string anyone along if nothing is to come of it.

If you don't want to date, then I would like to ask Emily out. That's if and only if you are okay with that. She has shown interest in me lately and it comes down to two great girls that I would regret letting either get away. At the same time, I would not wish to hurt either of you. If you decide you feel the same, let me know by the end of this week.

- Paul

The letter was dated the Saturday before Labor Day.

If she had only known, then she would not be in this predicament. The night with Nigel, the pregnancy scare, the fight with Emily, all would have been avoided. Sarah dropped the letter to her bed and lowered her head. A stream of tears flowed down her face, puddled on the sheets, and splotched the ink.

Memories from the weekend at the beach sifted in her head. When they had lost the bet, Paul had said he would also take a loss and run with her and Emily. She felt like that weekend had been a turning point. If she had only seen the letter, she might never have gone streaking, they never would have seen each other naked, and her values would have never faltered. Her actions over the past few months were far from pristine, and the intentions that Paul had shown proved there were still honorable guys.

If only she could return to the beach, sink her toes amongst the grains of sand, lay back on her towel, lie baking in the sun for some time, have the need to look into her purse for a loose piece of gum, see the note that hid within, and read the words. Then she would have known. Then she could have chosen differently. If only she could return to the beach.

Without hearing Emily out, Sarah had denied her effort to make amends. Why? Hurt, anger, remorse. All these feelings were based on the situation, but really, as she looked at the tear-streaked paper, all she felt was regret for failing to forgive and let go. She regretted her decision to neglect her and Emily's friendship. The painful past was too much to handle. The drowning regrets spoke truth to "Be angry yet do not sin."

If she was to be angry and not forgive, she might need Emily later, but she would not be there. She needed to talk to Emily and Paul, right the tension between them. She would worry about Nigel afterward, but Emily's friendship was at stake.

The first call for church on Sunday mornings echoed the halls at nine. Matty stood admiring his Sunday best in the mirror before Sarah picked out an outfit. Peering into her closet, she thumbed through her dresses. Girls at her church customarily wore skirts or dresses that fell below the knees with shoulder-width straps. Each hanger carried potential except the white Easter dress. The woven cotton embraced a purity that only the garment could possess. With each passing, the selection narrowed until she settled on a plain blue dress that embodied her present mood. A matching sweater cloaked the shoulders to complete the ensemble.

Sarah's church sat perched between a creek bed and a dusty gravel road. The hundred-year-old construction stood the test of time since being established in the 1800s. Numerous similar churches scattered the neighboring rural communities, all sharing unified beliefs.

Throughout the service, Sarah's concentration strayed from the preacher. Her mind debated what to tell Emily and Paul, and anticipating their reactions. The sermon only reached her ears when the preacher read about a man who wandered out into the wilderness and prayed to die. The story probably stuck out because she considered dying being easier than forgiving her friends, retracting the lies, and facing herself.

The dismissal of church, lunch, and later parts of the day clouded together in a fog as she packed for school. As she arranged her belongings, Cliff appeared from the hall. "Hey, Sar. I'm going to miss you. You'll be back at Christmas though, right?"

"Yeah; of course, Dad." She turned from her luggage, arching to wrap her arms around his neck.

"Everything going alright at school? I know we haven't spent much time talking since the semester started."

"Yeah, Dad, I am fine; just a little burned out from the way the season ended. Finals are coming up as well, so that adds to the stress."

"Okay. Well, if you need me to help with anything, I certainly can."

"That's alright. I appreciate it, but I will just be studying."

"Okay. I checked the oil and the tires, so your car should be good. I can change the oil when you get back."

"Thanks, Dad." Seeing him out, she toppled to her bed in disgust, her face in the pillow. The lies were proliferating.

The drive felt shorter than usual, as anxiety quicken the trip with her thoughts. She usually drove with the radio accompanying the ride, but this trip was different. This time, she barely noticed the cars around her. This time felt different.

The winding roads that approached the mountain and Beval pulled Sarah away from her trance. Topping the hill revealed the main hall on campus backed with a misty mountain range. Dark clouds and impending rain from the distance outlined the horizon. Her foot slipped from the brake in a surge to beat the rain.

As Sarah pulled into the spot next to Emily's car, she quickly unloaded her belongings. Turning the key while strapped with bags, the door opened to a dark and desolate apartment.

"Odd. Emm, are you here?" Nothing. "Hey, Emily, I am back. I wanted to see if we could talk."

Still nothing. Sarah checked the couch and kitchen before snooping through Emily's room. Emily's watch lying on the nightstand instigated the worry that something was wrong.

Dashing down the stairs, Sarah checked the notepad hooked on the door, but nothing. *Maybe she went to eat. Maybe she was staying with Paul. Maybe she went to the library.* With all these possibilities, Sarah was frantic to drive around in search for Emily.

Reaching for her keys, she opened the door to go back out, but walking up the sidewalk was Ralph. He started running toward her. He had been crying. The keys dropped from her hand and she paled as he began to tell her what happened the night before.

CHAPTER 17:

The Night Before

P aul's truck had only been for sale a few days before receiving an offer. With the call came a deep sadness. The man would drop the money off the following day. Paul and the secondhand Chevy's six-year relationship endured first dates to his first kiss, sharing every notable milestone in between. However, with a slipping transmission and no money for repairs, he decided to salvage what money he could while the truck ran. Along with this rush of emotions came the subtle thought of having one last ride through town before handing over the keys. A solo escape only painted a lasting memory of gloomy nostalgia. Ultimately, he drove to Emily's. Only after a few knocks at the door did her face appear. "Sure, that sounds great. I just got out of the shower, so give me a few minutes. I'll be ready by the time you get settled on the couch."

Edging the pavement, he braked before turning into the lot of the convenience store. The pump ran, clicking the dials as Emily went inside the store. Paul's heart tugged with each gallon that siphoned through the hose. Seeing Emily coming through the doors, he wiped his face with his sleeve before flashing a smile. Emily pulled a pack of gum from the cusp of her back pocket as she cornered the truck bed.

"Would you like a piece of gum?" she offered.

"Thanks, Emm." Tucking the gum back between the pocket seams, she nestled her head against Paul's shoulder. A resonating pop from the pump caused him to lift his arm. Emily turned away, but Paul reached out and pulled her back. He opened his door, ushering her to climb in.

"Alright, fasten your seatbelt," teased Paul. Emily slid closer, reaching over her shoulder, blindly fumbling for the seatbelt, her eyes still fixed on Paul.

Paul circled Main Street, leading out of town. The truck climbed to the top of the hill that hosted the iconic view of the city before cresting the top. Their concentration on each other more than conversation curbed their attention from the rattle from beneath the truck. Breaking his trance, his next idea was to give her a slight kiss on the lips. The kiss persisted for only a few seconds, but an eternity hung among them. Paul never saw the car stopped at the red light. The two were still locked together when the glass began to scatter around them. As the shards flew and the tires screeched, pieces floated through the cabin until they shuddered to a halt. Despite the severity, both only suffered minor scratches, until the semi-truck hardly braked before ramming into Paul's Chevy. Then everything went dark.

Paul's eyes flew open. The last, fleeting memories spun in his head. *Where were the people he hit? Where was he? Where was Emily?* Paul snapped the monitor cords, IVs, and oxygen ports before swiveling to the side of the bed and pummeling down to the floor. With all of his strength, Paul crawled through the hall, frantically examining every room.

"Where's Emily?! Where is she?!" An older man occupied the first room, presumably the truck driver. The next was a middle-aged lady who was covered with bruises. She had to have been in the car he hit. For a small town, there wouldn't be but a handful of people in the emergency room, but still no Emily. The nurses, hearing the commotion, rushed to restrain Paul from further injuring himself.

"Where is she?!" he demanded.

"She, she ..." started the nurse, but before she could finish, Paul screamed in terror.

CHAPTER 18:

Choices

A small, conventional clock ticked off its rhythm, perched on the wall overseeing the waiting area of the hospital. Silence filled the air. Occasional bursts of pandemonium jolted the room whenever the swinging doors leading to the operating room flung open. Near the entrance hunched a small girl. Her hands covered the front of her face. Tears gradually streamed between her fingers and trickled down the side of her face.

She had become so accustomed to the interruptions in the tranquil air that the opening doors no longer made her jump to her feet. It wasn't until the doctor called Emily's name that Sarah made any motion.

"Emily Ellis … Are you a friend or family member of Emily's?" She was the only one his voice addressed. Emily's parents lived on the other side of the state and would not arrive for another few hours, while Ralph and Abby had left to get some rest.

"Family," she fibbed. "Is she okay? Is she awake?" The doctor swallowed hard. Sarah could tell he had given similar talks many times before, but this was a different situation.

"She is not awake … we had to put her into a medically induced coma. The swelling on her brain is dangerously high, so we needed to decrease the blood flow to the area." He took a long pause, followed by a deep breath. "We don't know if she will be alright or not."

Sarah began to cry again. The doctor leaned over and gave her a hug.

"Can I see her?" Sarah asked, a plea of desperation.

"Of course. I will walk you down."

The long white hallway of the wing seemed endless. Reaching Emily's room midway down the corridor seemed like a years-long journey. When they finally approached the doorway, the doctor excused himself, "You're welcome to speak with her. We often believe they can still understand while comatose."

Emily's face was bruised black and blue, her nose broken. After being rear-ended, the second impact launched them into the air, rolling five times before halting upside down. No movement came from within. Paul and Emily had to be extracted by the firefighters and removed on stretchers.

Sarah stood hunched over her best friend, watching her cling to life. Quivering and short of breath she whispered, "Why, why did this happen?" All she could think about was the last time they spoke. Emm had apologized, but Sarah refused to listen.

Sarah knelt beside the hospital bed and laid her head on the mattress. She'd rather this be her. She'd rather they had not fought. It was too late to talk with Emily. If only she could apologize. If only she could give her another hug and say she still loved her. If only. Despairing and alone, a still, soft feeling filled the air. Sarah looked up toward the ceiling and begged for just one more opportunity, one more chance to make things right. As she groveled, the still feeling consumed her body and a calm peace replaced the stifling agony that claimed her heart. She knew Emily was saved when she was an eleven-year-old girl. Her testimony was pure of grace with a time and a place where Jesus bestowed salvation. No matter the outcome, Sarah would see Emily again one day after a while.

As she rose from her knees, Sarah sat alongside of the bed, nose running, and eyes saturated and puffy. She looked around for a tissue box, but the counters were bare.

As she leaned back to compose herself, a bump followed by a knock came at the door. "Come in," she sniffled. A man in a wheelchair pushed his way through the door, rolling a wheel with one arm and fighting the retracting door with the other. Sarah rushed to assist him in the struggle. Not until she closed the door behind did she recognize Paul's tattered face. "Oh my gosh, Paul. Are you okay?" She fell, clasping him in her arms.

"Ouch! Easy, Sarah. I have internal bruising."

"I am so sorry, Paul. I—" but he interrupted before she could continue.

"It's fine. The doctor says that part will heal. The other is what I am concerned about."

With an inquisitive expression, reality sunk in as Sarah looked down at Paul, sitting .... "Paul, you don't think, you mean—"

"They say I have about a fifty–fifty chance of walking again, normally it's much less. There was a lot of damage, internal bleeding, but they think walking again is the least of my worries. The accident could have been worse. I am just worried about Emily. What have they said? This is the first time I've been permitted to visit."

"She is in an induced coma right now. They are afraid she might have brain damage. If she was awake, it might get worse. The only thing they can do is wait. If they try to operate, the chances of success are low."

A long silence followed in anticipation for the remainder of the update.

"And if she doesn't come out of the coma?"

"The longer she remains unconscious, the more likely she is brain … dead. Life support was connected because they are unsure if she can fully function otherwise."

"What about her parents?"

"They are on their way. It took the hospital a while to get in contact with them," she said. And then, after a moment's pause, she added, "Paul."

"Yeah, Sar."

"Did Emily say anything about me to you?"

"She didn't, but I asked about you the other day, and from what I could tell, something happened between you two."

"Yeah, but first I must tell you something. I found your letter over the break."

"Oh. My letter."

"To be honest, I had the same feelings toward you. I just never thought you felt that way," Sarah explained.

"Sar, I don't think this is the time to talk this over given Emily's…"

"I know. I know, but we had a fight before the break. You see, Emily knew I had a crush on you, but I had been seeing Nigel."

"So, why did you have an issue with us being together if you were dating him?"

"He asked me on a date, and I didn't know about the letter. I figured going on a date wasn't a big deal."

"Right, but it seems like you had more than just a date."

"What do you mean?"

"I think you need to talk to Nigel."

"Paul, I saw you and Emily in the bathroom the night of the party. I was so upset, and Nigel was the one person I could turn to."

"Oh, you saw us?" he murmured.

"Yeah, your shirts were off, and you were making out."

Paul lowered his head. "You're right, we were; but it didn't go any further than that. We had no intentions of … we were caught up in the moment. Emily stopped right after. She said you liked me and that we couldn't continue until she talked to you."

"She stopped?"

"Yeah."

"What makes you say that Nigel and I were doing more than just dating?"

"Well, while the party was raging, after Emily and I left the bathroom, we went back to the living room. She lay down on the couch and fell asleep. Someone handed me a shot and when I took it, I immediately started gagging. I tried to go back to the bathroom, but someone was inside, so I used Nigel's. When I came out, I saw you two lying there, naked."

Sarah shuddered at the word.

"Wait, we were just lying there?" Sarah asked.

"Yeah, I guess you just finished having sex and fell asleep."

"What makes you think we had sex?"

"Well that's usually what happens between naked people. But like I said, you were asleep when I came in."

"Paul…"

"Yeah, Sar."

"About that …" she continued.

"Look, Sarah. You don't have to explain. I know you were upset and likely did something you'd rather not care to remember."

"That's the thing though. I don't remember. I remember wanting to and that's it. When I woke up the next day, we were both naked, and I got up and left. I haven't spoken to Nigel, but well, I ended up being late."

"Late? You mean, you are…?"

"No. I know now I am not pregnant, but I'm still rattled by the thought of not knowing what happened."

"I do a good bit of running with Nigel, or used to. He never brought it up, nor did I mention anything. However, I did tell Emily about finding you. I felt like she needed to know. Emily said she was going to talk to you after the party, but things had been weird. I finally told her what I saw, and that I didn't think there was much reason for us not to date."

"Oh no! What did she say?"

"She was upset that she wasn't hearing about Nigel from her best friend."

"I know, I should have told her, but I was really upset. I thought I was pregnant. Paul, I was even having pains in places I thought could only be explained from having sex. I could not tell for sure though, because, well I had never had sex. When I collapsed after the race, the doctor told me I was severely anemic, and the immense pain and my late period …"

"I get it, and I know she was scared to mention us, too," Paul said. "And, Sarah, I'm sorry about not coming to visit in the hospital. Coach wanted us to go home. We could have fought him, but Emily and I thought it would only upset you seeing us."

"Paul, it's alright, I get it. I am sorry too," said Sarah, adding, "What now?"

"Well, I think it's best if we wait to see what happens to Emily. I don't want to talk about her like she isn't here. I care about you both so much."

"Paul can I ask you a question?"

"Sure."

"Do you think of me as a bad person after seeing Nigel and me together in bed?" she asked.

But Paul just looked at her, pondering over his choice of words.

"Be honest," insisted Sarah.

"Sarah, I am not going to lie to you. I have always thought of you as a great girl, and anyone would be lucky to have you. When I saw you lying there, I was shocked because I couldn't believe my eyes. It definitely made me question things, and yes, I do think you have changed."

Sarah hung her head.

"I have always imagined myself ending up with a woman that embodies your beliefs. However, we all do things we regret, but we are creatures of habit. I still see you as the shy girl from when we first met. I just hope that's who you still are."

Sarah lifted her head. "I am sorry, Paul." She gave him soft embrace before passing to leave.

"Sarah."

"Yeah, Paul?"

"One more thing before you go. Not for my sake or anyone else's, but I think you need to talk to Nigel."

She shook her head silently as she walked out into the hall.

Paul's requests failed to change her car's route. But as her pencil tapped on the desk, she wondered blankly over class notes. No amount of studying could detour her thoughts from Emily's future or Paul's advice.

"You need to talk to Nigel."

Talk to Nigel, she thought. They only spoke once since the party, and neither addressed the obvious awkwardness between them. Would she talk to him frankly about the sex, or what happened that night? Both struck cold to the bone.

CHAPTER 19:

Certain Truth

The rest of the week, after Sarah encountered Paul at the hospital, crawled by. Still unable to persuade herself, she remained unsure if the truth was really what she wanted to hear. If she had hooked up with Nigel, would knowing make the situation better?

Each day, Sarah visited Emily after class. Her condition, from the doctor's report, neither worsened nor progressed. Sarah struggled with the uncertainty of not knowing if Emily would get better or ... the unthinkable.

The visits were limited, she only stayed an hour before leaving to prepare for finals, but all her efforts to study seemed fruitless. Her grades had slipped to a pivotal point, where finals could determine if she passed.

The hospital transferred Paul to a new wing of the facility, stripping him of the ability to visit Emily. Physical therapy was ordered to keep his muscle mass intact. If he regained movement in his legs, the doctors wanted to prevent muscle loss and help him rebuild his strength more quickly. Not having confronted Nigel and with no news from Emily, Sarah refrained from seeing Paul.

Visitation at the hospital ended promptly at seven every night. By Thursday, Sarah had two more finals for the week, and she needed a B on one test to pass the class. However, there was only one way of chancing a high enough grade. She had already pushed her usual visitation with Emily well past the hour mark—nearing three hours—and seven o'clock. Sarah had decided that if she was going to make it through the last of her finals, she must talk with Nigel. Looking at the clock one last time, she gathered her strength to rise from the chair she had guarded all afternoon. If she didn't dare now, this would be the last opportunity before Nigel left for the semester.

Slowly, she walked down the hallway, to the elevator, and out to her car. The chill of the night caught her by surprise, as she had arrived when the sun still cast a warm glow. Now, darkness covered the town. Starting the engine, she fixed her hands on the wheel, pausing for a few breaths before moving her hand to the gearshift. She knew the way to his house.

Pulling onto the street, she parked short of his drive. *Am I going to think any less of myself? Will I cry in front of Nigel? No*, she refused. She might be hurt, but no matter what, she would not shed a single tear. If she was no longer a virgin, that would be her fault, not his, and she would have to live with whatever that meant.

Amassing her composure with each step up the walk, she saw Nigel's bike parked beside his car. No noise came from inside the house, but a few lights beamed though the windows. Knocking firmly, she waited until Nigel appeared. His face bore no sign of shock or surprise. Instead, his charming smile flashed across his face. "Sarah, what's up?"

"Hey. Can I come in?"

"Uh… yeah, sure."

Sarah stepped over the threshold into the all-too-familiar foyer.

"My roommate and his girlfriend are watching television on the couch. We can go up to my room though."

Her heart stuttered at those words, but this time, she meant business and nothing more.

The room was just as she remembered, unkempt, the bed unmade, clothes thrown about the floor, and the chest of drawers overflowing with socks and underwear. Upon seeing the sty, flashbacks from the party stormed her head. Her body entangled with Nigel's, her bra thrown to the floor, unbuttoning their pants. Her eyelids flickered to break the trance.

"Here, have a seat," he said, piling the clothes to the side.

"No thanks. I'll stand."

"Suit yourself." He settled on the edge looking up at her. To avoid further recurrences, Sarah sighed and sat beside him on the bed.

"Nigel, we need to talk."

"Okay. What do you want to talk about?"

"I think you know why I am here … You remember the night of the Halloween party?"

"Yeah. Sure."

"Well, I know we had a heated night and things got out of hand. Then we ended up naked, and well you know…" A long pause lingered as she finished.

"So what? We were naked," Nigel added.

"Yeah, naked, and we had sex and I thought I was pregnant!" she exclaimed.

Nigel scooted further away, onto the bed. She had not meant to unload all at once, especially the pregnancy scare.

"Whoa, whoa, whoa! You're pregnant?!"

"No. I thought I was because after the party I was late. I finally had blood work, which came back negative. Did we even use protection that night?"

"Protection? No, we did not use protection."

Sarah's eyes widened and she drew her hand, slapping Nigel across the face.

"How dare you sleep with a girl without having the decency to wear a condom, and not even talk to me afterward? You jerk! Do you realize what this could have done? I know I am just as guilty as you are, but don't guys keep those in their nightstand just in case?"

Still rubbing his cheek, Nigel interrupted. "Sarah, calm down."

"I will not calm down. If you cared about me, then you should have at least been prepared."

"Let me talk for a second," Nigel said.

Sarah sat back with her hands crossed over her chest, her breathing elevated. Her eyes felt full and puffy as she dammed the tears.

"Look, I do have some in my nightstand," he began.

Her mouth dropped open in astonishment, and she slapped him with her other hand.

"But we did not have sex," he continued.

"What?"

"No. After we took our clothes off, I leaned over to my nightstand but fell out into the floor. I thought you knew because when I came to, I crawled back in bed and you were already asleep."

"So, we didn't?"

"No. I cannot fathom how we could have. Are you thinking of some-one else?"

"No. I had just assumed. And when I woke up the next morning, I had a lot of pain down there, and I thought, but wait …," Sarah paused, "If you were not talking to me after the party because I was a one night stand, then why didn't you say anything?"

"For starters, I figured you knew I passed out in the floor, and secondly, I was pretty embarrassed by the thought of you and Emily laughing behind my back. Heck, I couldn't even bring myself to tell my friends," said Nigel.

"You didn't tell anyone?"

"No, did you?" he asked.

"Obviously not, but Paul found out," she added.

"How in the world?"

"You remember asking me about throwing up in your bathroom?"

"Yeah."

"Well, Paul told me the other day that it was him. He saw us after he left the bathroom. He said the only person he told was Emily."

Nigel pondered before speaking, "I guess this means everything is good then, right?"

"I suppose, but what are we going to do now?" Sarah replied.

"We?"

"Yeah, are we going to be a couple, or just friends, or what?"

"Sar, we are teammates, so we will always be friends. As far as us though, I am going away next semester for an internship. I know we are probably not in the best position right now, but I'd rather not start or postpone anything. It just doesn't make sense. I am glad you are okay, though. I was worried when they carried you to the hospital, but I figured I wouldn't help matters by coming to see you."

Sarah stared down at her hands, trying to understand what he was saying.

"I guess this is it? You're leaving for Christmas tomorrow and will be gone when I get back?" she inquired.

"Yeah. I'm sorry I didn't mention it before. I just finalized my plans about a week ago; by that point, we weren't talking."

"No; I understand."

Nigel leaned in to give her a hug. With a last embrace, she left the bed for the door. "Goodbye, Nigel."

"See ya, Sarah."

She had reached out, gone past her limits, and let someone in. Now she floated to the car, feeling empty. Her chances with Paul were gone and Nigel was leaving. On one hand, she was thankful nothing happened that night, but the circumstances were merely luck. On the other, she was crushed. The three people she cherished most were gone. She sought an answer, and received the closure she needed, but the answer was not what she expected. It was closure anyone should be thankful for, but not in that moment.

Sarah dropped the keys on the table, but she did not pick up her books or look over her notes, nor did she try washing her sorrows away in the shower. Instead, she buried herself under the bed covers. *Who am I now, and what's next?*

Wanting to drown the memories from the past month, she considered throwing up, running away, or even transferring schools. As all three thoughts crossed her mind, she stumbled back on the patterns of the black butterfly.

Her eyes shot open as a rustle of excitement filled the night air, breaking her from her night terror. The boys from next door had wandered over to the girls' apartment on the other side to celebrate finishing the semester. The lightning that crackled harmlessly outside in the night sky was heard in teasing echoes between bashing gusts of wind.

A summons from the bed directed her hand to the bathroom light. She gazed deeply in the mirror at her reflection. She gently slid open the cabinet drawer and blindly placed her hand on the scissors. Without breaking her stare, she brought them to the sink. Gulping shallow breaths, Sarah reached down into her gym bag, retrieving the hair tie she had once tossed aside. Slowly she twirled her hair into a ponytail, and then pulled the locks down to the left side of her face. Tears pooled as she laced her fingers through the scissors and clipped away at the fine threads. Snip by snip, the fibers split, her eyes threaded closed until the resistance was sliced through. Opening her eyes, she struggled to comprehend the altered reflection. Her once-beautiful hair now fell just in line with her jaw.

Throwing the scissors on the counter, Sarah stepped back to examine the result. Her work was uneven, reckless. Anyone would easily acknowledge this was her own work.

There was nothing that could keep her from being noticed now. A brief lapse in sanity commandeered the scissors, cutting strands with no way of masking the mistake. *Hideous.* She thought a new style would change her, for it would not be the same locks tied behind her head in a pony tail that Nigel had run his fingers through, nor the strands she cherished throughout the semester, or the hair she blacked out with on the regional course. Other girls had shortened their hair after a breakup, and she thought the change in their appearance helped them cope. No matter, Nigel would not see her like this. He would be gone. With one final look of disgust, she turned off the bathroom lights and went back to bed.

The noise from the party next door continued as she tried to drift off. She wondered if some girl was making the same mistake she had made: self-loathing, seeking comfort, and confiding in someone she trusted by giving herself away. She tried to wipe the thoughts out of her mind. There was nothing she could do. Restlessly, Sarah turned over on her side catching a glimpse of the clock. It was 11:37.

CHAPTER 20:

One Bed

L ethargy tugged at Sarah with the dread of two final exams. Her focus dwindled to the ground to avoid being noticed. She contemplated tucking her hair under the rim of a hat, but the direct attention to her head by wearing a hat would only draw notice to her hair. Luckily, the bareness of the dining commons assured her that almost everyone had finished their exams prior to Friday.

Sarah had been instructed by her doctor to increase her red meat and leafy greens intake to ensure adequate iron in her diet. Heading to the corner for an omelet filled with steak bites, bacon, peas, carrots, and some spinach proved more intentional than convenient. Watching for the egg to fry, a cartoonish voice she recognized from last spring interjected.

"Sarah?"

"Hi, Melody. Looks like you got stuck with a Friday test too," she said, directing the conversation.

"Yeah. Stinks, doesn't it? I almost didn't recognize you. When did you get your hair cut so short?"

"Oh, I just recently donated it, you know with Christmas coming up," she fibbed.

"Oh, that's so sweet. It looks good on you."

"Order up!" said a voice over theirs.

"Well, thanks, and good luck on your exams," Sarah said.

"You, too," replied Melody.

Without dawdling, Sarah walked to the coffee station. She didn't know Melody well, but she could detect the sarcasm.

Cup and tray in hand, she sought refuge in a nook. Real honesty was one thing, but a near stranger's fake compliment was miserable. Covering her face with the palm of her hand, she shoveled the eggs into her mouth. More students were pouring through the entryway. She would be early for her exam, but she'd rather wait buried inside her coat on the floor for her first class.

The pencil marks came in waves, working through the problems on hunches. The caffeine from the breakfast coffee dissipated, leaving only fumes to burn. Her mind stumbled on each question, but somehow she managed to put pencil to paper. Only she, another student, and the professor remained when her pencil dropped to the desk. Sarah scuttled out the side of her chair, thankful to hand in her paper.

"Have a Merry Christmas, Sarah, and here, take a candy cane," said the professor.

"Thank you. Merry Christmas to you as well," Sarah replied. A slight yet foreign smile crossed her face at Dr. Donaldson's generosity.

Pausing long enough to stuff the candy into her backpack, she continued outside to the greeting of a cool gust of air. The wind whipped though her hair. Instinctually, she threaded her fingers past her ear to bunch the strands together, but it lacked the length. A single tear beaded at the crest of her nose but was met by a clinched sleeve.

When she took a seat for her next test, Sarah shed her coat, draping the bundle over the side rail. An unfamiliar warmth churned in the room. "Sorry, class, the thermostat broke, and unfortunately, the heater will not turn off."

At least no one will be worried about my hair, Sarah thought.

"You can go ahead and start; then, feel free to leave as soon as you finish," the professor continued.

Working through the questions, Sarah gained confidence with each answer. Each mark indicated a step closer to completing the semester. Not sure how she reached the conclusions, trudging through the exam left her pulling from deep within her subconscious.

Placing her pencil to the desk, she slumped back. It was over—she could move on, put the semester behind, and focus on continuing with life. She glided from the room to the stairs and through the front doors. She pulled her jacket on in anticipation of the cold air. However, the presence of the sun made it a fair weather day. She knelt at a nearby bench, unstrapping her backpack. She removed the jacket, stuffing the fluff around her books. Fastening the zipper, she pulled the straps over her shoulders. The weight wore lighter, despite the bulk that tugged at the seams. A renewed view shielded her peripherals, concealing Nigel's approach. She froze while her intuition begged her to run. As Nigel changed his glance from an overlooked quarter, her heart skipped a beat.

"Oh! Hey, Sarah." exclaimed Nigel.

With an immense effort, she faked a composed appearance. She had no intention of feigning otherwise.

"Hey."

"Sorry, I almost didn't recognize you. Your hair…," he said.

"Yeah, just trying something new and easier," she winced at her lapse in story. "Much less maintenance."

"Well I always liked your long hair, but this is nice."

"Oh, thanks."

"Well, I've got to be going. I don't want to be late. Adios."

"Bye," she whispered, but he was already gone.

Nice. I liked your long hair. Could he have been more humiliating? She'd rather he said she looked hideous than that her old look was better. Terrible she could cope with. All the excitement and relief from finishing the semester faded. Instead of stopping to enjoy lunch, she decided to leave, go home, and disappear from Beval for the next four weeks. But she couldn't, not yet anyway.

She needed to check on Emily, but first a detour by their apartment. *Our?* The statement felt ghostly since she now lived there alone.

The inside had the same eerie silence as a hotel absent of guests for decades. *All the more reason to go home,* she thought. Second-guessing her return for dirty laundry, she hurried to retrieve the basket, almost toppling down the stairs in her angst to leave.

Most of the city was vacated for the break. Only a few cars traveled the roads and were likely the locals. A red light caught Sarah just before making the turn to the hospital. The signal rotated through its motions for a lone car to pass. Finally, the light turned green then to yellow as she drove underneath.

Aside from an elderly couple sitting under an "It's a boy" balloon tethered to the seat, the waiting area was vacant. From their appearance, Sarah figured they had stayed though the night hoping to welcome their new grandson. Sarah signed her name on the check-in sheet provided by the attendant; the lady didn't need to ask who she was visiting. Heading toward the elevators, a doctor scurried past, likely the stork who delivered the baby.

Her thoughts were still imagining the excitement of the family as she turned a corner, ramming into an unsuspecting person. The man, unfazed by the collision, kept Sarah from being knocked to the floor.

"Sorry," she said, shaking her head.

A dimpled face marked with concern met her eyes.

"Hi, Sarah! You know, we really have to stop meeting when you are having trouble staying on your feet." Pulling away as she regained her balance, Sarah pondered over where she knew him from.

"Michael?"

"The one and only," he laughed.

"What are you doing here?" she asked.

"I am doing my physical therapy rotation here. I just started last week, hoping to land a job with the hospital. What about you? Are you getting those legs checked or visiting someone?"

"Actually, I am visiting my roommate. She was in a car accident and has been in intensive care."

"Oh, Sarah! I am so sorry." Michael leaned over to give her a hug. "If there is anything you need, I will be around."

"Thanks. It has been tough, but I am just visiting before I leave for Christmas break," she paused. "I'll let you get back to work."

Michael smiled. "Nice seeing you again, Sarah."

"You too," she said, turning to the elevator.

By the ping of the fifth floor, Sarah began to question herself. *I should have brought flowers; such a terrible friend. What if she woke up today? I guess I could swing by the gift shop.* Before deciding to turn around, Sarah noticed Emily's parents, Carter and Cora. Her mother's head rested on his chest as Carter stroked her hair.

"Sarah," said Cora sniffling.

"What's wrong? Is Emily still stable?"

"Sarah, we have some bad news … The doctors came in an hour ago and said there was nothing else they can do for Eme. We have been talking it over and there are no other choices at this time."

"What do you mean?"

"Sarah we are going to have to take her off …."

"No, you can't. She is still alive; she will get better," Sarah cried.

"Sarah, I know; I know. It will be okay. She'll be better off." The two women began sobbing together.

Choked up, Emily's mom continued. "We want to spend one last Christmas with Eme, so we are going to keep her on until the day after Christmas. We have to keep her here though, so we cannot move her closer to home."

"Can I see her now?" Sarah asked.

"Of course. But I want to say; we don't want you spending your whole break here. I know you want to see her, but there isn't any use in making yourself sick worrying about her anymore."

Sarah wanted to confess how badly she needed to apologize, and how she wished they had never fought the last time they talked, but she kept silent. She knew it would only upset Cora more.

"Do you mind if I spend the night with her tonight, and then leave tomorrow? It has just been crazy the past week, and I would really like to have one last night by her side."

Emily's parents exchanged looks of approval. "Certainly, dear. We will stay at the hotel for the night; get some rest and something to eat," Emily's mother said.

"We'll see you two in the morning," her father added.

After bidding Emily's parents goodbye, Sarah shut the door before leaning against the bed. Only the bandages attempted to hide the glow on Emily's skin, and the half smile she wore.

Sarah pulled a small wooden chair from against the wall. As she sat beside her beloved friend, she confessed her sorrows. "Emm, you're my best friend. I'll never lie or keep something from you again. Please don't leave me. Please."

Her voice initially quivered with sobs, but slowly, the stammer conceded to chuckles as she reminisced on the good times spent together. "You remember when we were at camp one year? The guys bet you couldn't climb a rope, and you said they would have to clean our bunk house for the whole week if you could? It sure was nice having our own personal maids. Oh, or the time when you did the milk mile, that was even better Emm," she laughed.

Emily was always the type of person to make things happen, and Sarah was going to miss that.

With a suppressed yawn, Sarah acknowledged the need for coffee. She scoured her purse and wallet for loose change for the café. There were a couple of quarters at the bottom, but the change was not what kept her from searching. Her fingers had landed on a small vessel. Withdrawing her hand, she pulled out a half-full bottle of fingernail polish. It was a dusky blue color.

"What a better way to spend the evening together than how we spend other nights alone, laughing, and enjoying stories while getting a mani–pedi." The lacquer was a little dry, but with a good shake, Sarah was able to revive the remainder. "Revive the remaining…," she repeated before remembering the origin, "Strengthen that which remains."

Is there something I need to do? Only a faint noise from a clock could be heard, but the slight tick was outside of her consciousness. Not until she set aside the quandary did peace arrive. However, the ambiguity of what the words meant lingered.

Sarah realized she was still holding the bottle of polish and gave another shake before unscrewing the top. Emily's hand already lay along her side, so Sarah pealed the sheets back enough to uncover her fingers.

Sarah delicately stroked the brush over the nails, tasking each stroke as if it were the last. With the slightest imperfection, she dabbed an alcohol wipe from the cabinet to remove the muck and start again. She tried not to think about the fact that Emily would be buried in this polish. Attempting to distract herself, Sarah continued telling Emily stories.

"You know what was really funny? One Sunday last year, you and I had gone out for a long run. We were far out, probably a good three miles from making it back to the parking lot when I tripped and twisted my ankle. I was so afraid we wouldn't make it before dark, so you tried to carry me," she laughed. "Then out of nowhere, Paul showed up. I climbed on his back and he ran with me the rest of the way. You were saying he couldn't do it, and he was bound to prove you wrong. I laughed so hard at you two bickering that I forgot about the pain. I just didn't say anything because we were having too much fun.

"You know, Paul really is a sweet guy. I know why you like him, and I cannot blame you for wanting to date him.

"I almost forgot to tell you. When I get back next semester, I have an appointment to see my doctor. I am hoping my iron levels are better so I can start running again. A second ferritin test will tell if I am in the clear. If not, I might have to miss part of the track season.

"I haven't decided if I should tell my parents about everything that has happened. With all the lies already, it is difficult to be honest. I know what you would say, 'Just tell them and if they don't like it, tough.' Sometimes, I wish I could be as bold as you, but then again, I think that's why I always had you around."

Sarah glanced over at the clock. It was already eleven. She yawned, unsure how much longer she could stay awake. She looked around to see if there was another pillow or a blanket. None of the cabinets held anything of use aside from the paper bed covers.

She looked over at Emily, listening for any noise from the hall, but no one was traveling the corridors. She assumed no more staff would stop by for the night either since the doctors had declared there was nothing else to be done.

The hospital bed would normally accommodate one person, but their bodies were half the stature of a grown man's. In the dorms, Sarah and Emily had shared a twin bed numerous times when one of their moms came to visit. To avoid knocking off any sensors, Sarah placed Emily's right hand on her own stomach, making just enough room. She crawled onto the bed and curled up next to Emily, her head propped on Emm's shoulder. The familiar smell generated even more fond memories from sharing beds and adjoining seats on the bus. She breathed in deeply. Letting her best friend go would be difficult. Knowing what tomorrow would bring, she fought off sleep just to lie in bed with Emily one final time. Sarah rolled over on her side to look at Emily's face. "Thanks, Emm, for always being there for me."

Her eyes drifted shut, and no longer able to elude sleep, she spent the last night ever with Emily.

As the sunrise prodded through the window of the hospital room, the beams stretched through the blinds to cast their presence on Sarah's face. It took her a moment to remember where she was; she was not accustomed to being awakened by the sunrise. She crept out of the bed, as if not to stir Emily from her slumber. The clock on the wall showed it was already seven thirty. Emily's parents would likely return any moment. She walked over to the sink to rinse her face. For what she was about to do, she did not want to be half asleep.

The moment had come that she had dreaded for weeks. She had thought about coming back to visit Emily over break, but ultimately, it would still be hard to say goodbye, and she wanted Emily's parents to have the remaining days with her. There was no use delaying; it was time. She walked over to the side of Emily's bed, unable to reframe her tears. She leaned over, giving Emily a hug she could hardly pull away from. She could hear the faint heartbeats as her head rested on Emily's chest. Emm had been so strong, her heart so powerful, but now she lay sleeping and waiting.

She gathered herself together. "I love you, Emily." At last, she bent over her friend. This time she placed her lips on top of Emily's forehead. Straightening, Sarah turned from the bed and sat back in the chair to slip on her shoes. When she finished tying her laces, she lifted the sheets over Emily, hiding her work and adjusting the covers to their previous arrangement.

She could not help but take another look at Emily. With a long sigh, Sarah reached out and turned the handle. She walked out, leaving the door to close behind her.

CHAPTER 21:

Home Sweet Home

H ints of sizzling bacon and pancake batter floated up from the
kitchen as Sarah straightened the comforter and fluffed her
pillows. To her, tucking the sheet corners in on each side served to keep
her from crawling back in bed during the day, or maybe to keep the
warmth sealed inside.

As she passed her brother's room, Sarah inched back and cracked the
door open. His head appeared lost, still buried in the pillow. By this time
of day, he would usually be wreaking havoc, but she knew her own rest-
lessness was to blame. Since returning home, sleepless nights welcomed
her, even though the semester was over. With her mind free to wander,
the suppressed emotions had unraveled after exams. To calm her thoughts,
she required Matty's presence past his bedtime to play games.

Poor kid, she thought. *Should I wake him up or let him sleep?* Only
after a second of hesitation did she settle on waking him. She shoved

open the door, catapulting onto the bed. "Get up, sleepy head. Mom is making breakfast, and I am going to eat all of yours."

His groan from being stirred turned into a panic, attempting to find his footing without being beaten to the table. The two barreled their way from the bed through the door, momentarily caught together in the frame before Matty broke free.

His sudden disappearance left Sarah in second place. Her delayed arrival to the kitchen resulted in Matty already sitting at the table with a plate full of pancakes.

"Who is slow now?" Matty bantered.

"Fine, fine; just don't get a stomachache from eating too fast," Sarah replied.

"Good morning, Sarah." Cliff was reclined in a chair alongside Matty, sipping his coffee while reading over the newspaper.

"Hey, Dad." She walked over to give him a hug and a kiss on the check. Circling the table, she ruffled Matty's hair before addressing her mom.

"This smells amazing."

Megan removed another stack from the stove and slid the honey over the counter.

"Here you go, Liv."

"Thank you, Mom."

The steaming plate had only grazed the placemat when Matty popped up. "I'm done!" he exclaimed, proceeding toward the kitchen to load his plate in the wash.

"Where do you think you are going?"

"Back to bed, of course. If no one else wakes me up." Sarah laughed and shook her head.

Eyeing the stairs until he was out of sight, Megan pulled out a seat across from Sarah. Her mom's obvious struggle to preface what she was about to say was explained by her next statement.

"Emily's parents called from the hospital," she said.

Sarah hadn't told her parents about Emm's situation. She had foregone any conversations about school, not just the wreck. She had never fathomed Emily dying, optimistic of a full recovery followed by her righting their quarrel.

"Sarah Olivia, why did you not tell us what was going on? I was speechless when they spoke as if we knew about the wreck," Megan continued.

"I am so sorry, Mom. I couldn't talk about it. The crash happened and I only found out after getting back to school. Then, I had exams to worry about. On my way home is when I was told their decision."

"Oh, Sarah. I am not mad at you. It was just a shock."

"Can we not talk about it anymore? I said my goodbyes to her before coming home, and I would just like to leave it at that," she begged.

"Sure; I understand," said Megan.

No one offered to initiate a different conversation until her dad refolded the paper. "*A Christmas Carol* is playing in town on Christmas Eve. What do you say we all go? It will be nice to get into the Christmas spirit."

He must have known the stretch of the gesture. As much as Sarah loved going to plays, her expression waivered far from excitement.

"That will be fine," she muttered.

"Great. I'll get the tickets today."

Distressed, Sarah carried her plate into the kitchen. "I think I am going to lie down for a little while."

"Okay, but don't sleep too long, or else you will be up late again tonight," said her mother.

Sarah disregarded her concern, but before edging the stairs, her dad called out. "Do you want to ride with me to get the tickets? I was going to take the Jeep out."

She stopped for a second to consider. Riding had to be better than lying in bed, tossing and turning. "Alright, I will go with you. Just let me change out of my pajamas."

The rattle of the starter carried from the carport. Sarah opened the side door, watching Cliff fidget under the hood.

"All set? Go ahead and climb in, I just need to adjust the carburetor," Cliff said.

Sarah tugged at the wedged handle before the door budged. The frigid vinyl seats seeped through her jeans, initiating a shiver. Placing one hand under her legs, Sarah ran the other along the dash. Her dad had bought the Jeep new before she was born. She remembered many times before her mom riding up front, while she and Matty nestled on the bench seat on Sundays, heading to church.

The day Sarah passed her permit test, Cliff handed over the keys, insisting she learn to drive a stick. Even though her Volkswagen was an automatic, she still enjoyed grinding the gears on the Jeep that summer after turning sixteen.

She took in a deep breath to refamiliarize herself with the dank cabin, aged seat covers, and original rubber floor mats. Even the lanyard that dangled from the mirror was faded from twenty years of sunshine. Unlike the inside, the exterior was coated with fresh paint, new tires, and aftermarket decals. She could imagine the Jeep new, but the memories wore more favorable.

A creak, followed by a well-timed slam of the driver's side door jostled the Jeep. Stretching out for the clutch and finding first, the two drove off in the direction of the theater. They were silent for most of the ride. The cabin always echoed from the roar of the road, the shifting of gears, and the clanking of metal from within. Even without Sarah daydreaming, most words were lost in the jumble.

Idling to a stop in the parking lot, Cliff switched off the engine. "Are you coming in or do you want to stay here?"

"I will just wait, if that's alright."

"That's fine. I will leave the keys with you."

After he was gone, Sarah settled back into her seat and closed her eyes. Uncertain whether sleep or a continuation of daydreams captured her consciousness, Sarah's stupor continued with memories of riding around, playing with her brother, going to church, and having ice cream on Friday nights. In a blink, however, her dad had returned with the tickets. She flung her eyes open when she heard the jostle at the door, then leaned over and popped the lock.

"I saw Ms. Kites, your first-grade teacher," Cliff said. Sarah's fondness for Ms. Kites lasted throughout grade school. On special occasions, Sarah had joined the children to read aloud, imagining being a teacher herself. Those delightful afternoons highlighted Sarah's day, but in the years since she had forgotten the warmth visiting brought.

"How is she doing these days?" Sarah asked.

"She's contemplating retiring; said thirty years meant it was time to hang up the eraser."

"She's already taught that long?"

"Well it's been, what, close to fifteen years since you had her? She'd love to see you and said to feel free and drop by anytime. Oh. And good thing we came ahead and got tickets. The attendant said they're almost sold out."

The Jeep fired up with the initial turn of the key, stuttering only slightly with the reverse gear. She had forgotten about Christmas. The elation that usually filled her heart was missing, replaced by the reminder that Emily's days on life support were shortly numbered.

The number of days until Christmas echoed in her head until they returned home. Closing the garage door behind them as the Jeep sputtered to a stop, Sarah thanked her dad for the ride and tickets. Undeterred, she passed through the living room and headed straight upstairs, not bothering to change or unmake the bed before lying down.

Despite the ease of a midmorning trip, exhaustion consumed her body to the bones. From what, she wasn't sure. Regardless of the quality, she had slept and exerted little energy during the day. Ever since the doctor's diagnosis, running and working out were replaced with sleeping, eating, and studying for exams. The core of the matter was, she wasn't tired in the sense of needing sleep, but of self-loathing.

As a child, Sarah was taught to avoid sinning. The problem then, however, was she always viewed sin as something bad that people did. *Is that the only type of sin? Gluttony is also a sin of over indulging. What did I think sleeping all the time and worrying about Emily and the pregnancy scare was?* Those things had lapsed and were decided. She couldn't live in the past anymore, refusing to move forward. She had to go on.

The desire to move burned within her loins, despite her forgotten running shoes and packed-away shorts. Irritated, Sarah flung boxes from the closet. Leaving the mess scattered across the floor, she stripped down to her bare skin and then yanked on a long-sleeved shirt and shorts. Grabbing her shoes and socks she called out, "I will be back in a bit, Mom."

The transition of moving her legs from walking to jogging felt unnatural. Not having run in a month, her body resisted the change. The doctor said she could resume running once a regular period occurred. Granted, the regularity was questionable, but Sarah didn't care. She needed to run, to push herself; worrying only left her stranded.

Breaking through and letting her concerns fall behind would be her sole focus, not wasting concern on an uncontrollable past. Sure, she made her share of mistakes. It was human to care for others, get hurt, and feel at fault.

Continuing to push the pace, she reached the end of her road and headed down along the river, the same path she spent hours running in high school. Each step brought agility to her feet and clarity to her mind. *A few miles are all I need.*

Running had always served as an anchor, providing self-worth, poise, and confidence, attributes that no matter how hard she tried would never manifest from a guy or a group of friends. However, the lack of reserve to lean on this passion had proven taxing. Without valuing herself or her own intentions, everything else was for naught.

The bridge spanning the river to the extended trails was Sarah's usual turnaround for a leisure run. Without breaking stride, she sprang from the bridge, disappearing into the dense forest. A whole track season lay ahead, and if she didn't recast her sights now, another upset was inevitable. Her legs continued to flow underneath, gliding over the well-beaten path. She resisted turning around. *Just a little further.*

The surprise ending of the trail brought her to laughter. There was something to be said for embarking on a three-mile run and abandoning the original plan. Positioned in the middle of nowhere, only she was accountable for the six-mile trek home.

Sarah only deviated from her pace after passing the imaginary banner strung from the mailbox. An hour and thirty minutes felt good on fresh legs. Slowing to a walk, she noticed her dad on a ladder at the far end of the house. As he stretched out dangerously over the bushes, Sarah took hold of the lower rungs.

"Finally decide to put the Christmas lights up?" she asked.

"You know me, Sarah. I like to get them up just in time to take them down," he laughed. "Where did you go? You've been gone a while."

"Oh, I just went for a run, hit a groove so it ended up longer than I expected. Let me change and I will come help."

The chill brought by the saturated clothes dissipated under the cover of jeans and a jacket. Heading downstairs, Sarah stopped by her brother's room. "Come on. I'm going outside to help Dad."

He leaped from the floor, coat in hand, and followed her outside. Although Matty was more concerned with chasing Daisy, Sarah untangled the lights before handing them off to her dad. A few wobbles from Cliff creeping to the top rung, where a label clearly read, "Not a step," left her fumbling from the lights to brace the ladder. She had missed spending time with her family while struggling at school. Regardless of all the tribulations, nothing ranked more important than being with them.

While hanging the last strand of lights, her mom leaned from the porch calling for lunch. Megan had prepared a feast more common as a typical supper. "I figured we could enjoy a big lunch and not rush tonight."

"What's tonight?" Sarah asked.

"We're going caroling in town," Megan replied.

"Sorry, I must have forgotten, but I'm famished."

Sarah arrived at the table last as everyone else started eating. Occupied with accommodating the unexpected meal, prayer was usually outside their lunch custom. That was okay though. Before lifting her fork, Sarah closed her eyes briefly to give thanks. Thanks, as she was truly grateful.

As night fell, Megan ushered Matty upstairs. Before bundling up to join the other carolers, Sarah opened her songbook. As she skimmed through the pages for a hymn to practice, a title caught Sarah's eye. It was not a Christmas song by any means, but she started to sing the chorus aloud. "I will arise and go to Jesus, He will embrace me in His arms; In the arms of my dear Savior, O there are ten thousand charms."

She lay the book aside, continuing to sing, carrying the melody as she finished getting ready. When she looped around to the chorus a second time, she stopped. She couldn't sing any more. The piece meant something to her, but the missing clarity rendered her speechless. After a few seconds, she proceeded with another song, *Hark, the Herald Angels Sing.*

Unaware of how well her voice carried, Sarah only took notice when her mother popped her head through the door. "You sound great, Liv, and ready for caroling."

Sarah smiled. "Thanks, Mom. I will be down in a second."

"Okay; bring your brother when you come." Megan ran her fingers by Sarah's face slipping her hair behind her ears. "How are you going to style your hair now?"

"I'll probably brush it and wear a toboggan for now."

Megan smiled before turning to leave.

Switching on the bathroom light, Sarah peered into the mirror admitting her hair looked pitiful. When she opened the drawer, her gaze fell past the brush onto a hair tie.

CHAPTER 22:

Christmas

T he arrival of Christmas seemed to take forever every year. Although the anticipation differed, this season was much the same. The last decorations hung on the tree branches, atop the mantle, and from the roof edge. Sheets of ice covered the shaded steps on the backside of the house, but a pillar of snow was the only lingering adornment to be hoped for. With all the other preparations made, they awaited the Christmas Eve play.

There was something about the script that drew hundreds of people in the town to the theater. Sarah often hoped she would have a Christmas Eve dream much like the haunting of the three ghosts, ending with the happy resolve of her being a better person. This year, however, she no longer desired this fantasy. The ghost had already visited, and now she was waking up.

While Sarah stood at her closet, Megan came in with her hands tucked behind her. "Do you know what you are going to wear tonight, Sarah?"

"Not yet. I have a few ideas I may try on to decide."

"Before you do, there is something I wanted to give you early. Your dad and I were talking, and you are not a little girl anymore. You haven't been, but we just refused to think you are a grown up." She pulled her hands out front, holding a small package.

"Oh, Mom, are you sure? I still see myself as your little girl."

"We're not disowning you," Megan laughed.

Sarah took the box and slowly began to pull the wrapping paper off. When she lifted the lid, two diamonds sparkled from within.

"We thought it was time you had your very own pair of diamond earrings," Megan said.

"Thank you. They are beautiful!" Sarah ran back to her closet. "I will have to find a fancier dress to go with these."

She laid two sweater dresses on the bed. "Which do you think I should wear—the black or red one?"

"Well, it is Christmas. I think the red one would be lovely." A ring from the house phone drew her mother to the door. "I will let you finish getting ready. See you downstairs in a bit."

Ecstatic, she placed the case on the wardrobe and began undressing before the door clicked shut. Lifting the hanger, Sarah held the elegant red garment in front of her. The material lay plush against her body. She couldn't remember the last time she had worn it. Without being able to train and overindulging in food, she had gained a noticeable ten pounds, capturing even her mother's attention and mild concern. Still downplaying the fact that she was anemic, Sarah had come up with another fib. She claimed Coach Cavlere noticed some burnout this season and advised time off to rekindle the desire. She doubted her mother had bought the story, but she sounded convincing all the same. Sarah bent over, carefully stepping inside the dress. As she pulled the straps to her chest and over her shoulders, the fabric stretched snugly. With a little effort, she slid the zipper along her spine to the clasp. The dress secured, she turned to check how the fit looked on her. The weight she had gained was well distributed. With a newly shaped pudge at her belly and genuinely plump breasts and rear, the dress filled out evenly. *I can handle having these curves*, she thought.

Sarah no longer had her previous girlish figure. Her eyes drew from her hips to her bust, and then her glimmer dimmed slightly as she saw her hair.

When she arrived home for Christmas break, she knew her parents disapproved of the new haircut. She stuck to the story of deciding to donate the hair and cutting it herself. Relentlessly, Megan insisted on taking her to have it properly styled. Without jeopardizing much of the remaining length, the salon attempted a fashionable look. The woman had done a decent job, but even that failed to mask Sarah's insecurity.

She looked down at the diamonds, picked them up, and threaded each through her ears. *At least I can show off my new earrings without all my hair covering them up.*

Satisfied, she reached into a drawer for a pair of black stockings. Not the color she would normally wear, but they would go best with her outfit. Propped against the bed, she pulled each over her heel. Slowly she guided each roll up her leg, careful not to cause a run. "I guess this really defeats the purpose of shaving my legs," she laughed, inching the stockings over her knees, content with their integrity. "Oh, shoes." The black heels with a velvet bow not only wore best with the stockings, but the three inches added lift without exaggerating her height. With a final look at her outfit, she turned to the door to leave.

Two routes led to the theater, one directly through town, while the other wound along the back roads. With time to spare, Cliff chose the scenic path adorned with Christmas lights and displays. The Jeep slowed at each house, pausing for the views. Matty loosened his seatbelt to adhere to the window, as Elvis softly caroled through the radio.

The nativity scenes and festive lights dwindled closer to town. In their place, hung an array of matching bulbs and strands with a practical feel. The monotonous view peeled Matty and the rest from the windows, as their attention channeled toward the theater.

Main Street's parallel parking lined the sidewalks full of cars. Arriving early to wait outside had spanned the minds of a considerable crowd. Roughly, a hundred people lined the walkway leading to the entrance. Sarah clutched her overcoat, anticipating the chilling night for late December.

As the Jeep door opened, the wind whipped beneath her arms. Sarah quickly flung the coat on before folding her hands under the sleeves until the breeze met the resistance of the crowd.

Matty grabbed her attention as he showed his ability to blow a double bubble with his gum. She refrained from popping it before he could start the second one. "See, I told you I could do it."

"That's really good, Matty. Maybe you can teach me when we get back…" Her response was cut short as she looked down the line. There, dressed in a black pea coat wearing a beanie that barely covered his brown hair was Wesley and his family. The two had not talked or seen each other in a few years. Thinking back now, she could not remember doing so since she left for college. Sarah stared in his direction, but her trance was broken when his awestruck eyes caught hers. Then she remembered her own hair, the likely cause of his surprised expression.

"Sarah?"

"Hi, Wesley."

"Wow, you look amazing. How have you been?" he asked, wrapping his arms around her. For a second, the embrace cloaked her memory of them ever being apart.

"Good. Just back from school for the semester. How about you?"

"I'm visiting the family for a few weeks, and then I will fly back out."

"Oh, did you move after graduating?"

"Yeah, I wanted to try somewhere new."

"Are we talking about the same person?" Sarah blurted before she could restrain herself.

"Ha! Yeah, but you know, a lot has changed in, well… the past few years."

She wondered if he was seeing anyone. To entertain the question would make for a desperate conversation, but she hadn't to wait long for the answer.

"That's true; things change quickly at this age," she said.

"Yeah, speaking of… Haley," he called over his shoulder. A beautiful blonde, bearing a resemblance to Sarah from a distance, greeted him with a kiss on the cheek. "Haley, this is Sarah, the girl I dated from high school. And Sarah, this is Haley, my fiancé."

Her stomach knotted up at the enduring word. "I've heard so much about you. Wesley, you do have good taste in women," stated Haley.

"He does," agreed Sarah. "Congratulations you two."

"Thanks, Sar. Hey, it was good seeing you. We are going to catch up with my parents."

"Nice to meet you, Haley," Sarah said.

"You as well," Hailey replied.

Sarah twisted to watch them walk away as Wesley slid his arm around Haley's waist. Her eyes twinkled with bliss for them. Wesley's sweet nature had left her believing for years he was the one; however, the couple she barely knew was meant to be. She gave a slight smile at the afterthought.

When she turned around, her dad leaned over, whispering, "You alright, Liv?"

"Yeah, Dad, I'm fine," she said as she cast another smile. She never thought she would feel happy for her first love to find someone else, but in a satisfying way, she was. Moreover, she was glad they had stopped to talk. She could remember after they had broken up, how she prayed for things to work out between them. Even though they were not together, she found her answer that night.

The line began to shuffle ahead of them as the doors finally opened. Sarah took a seat near the end of the aisle, next to her brother. A small stage took up the center of the community playhouse, opening with a dim light that brightened to reveal Scrooge. *How terrible*, she thought. *He spends his remaining years pushing people out of his life, all because of a dramatic past. He loved and lost, but never learned to live afterward.*

Matty nudged her on the shoulder. "Do you want some popcorn?"

"Thanks." Reaching for the tub, Sarah wondered how much of the story he really understood, or if this was just a Christmas play depicting ghosts. Undoubtedly, he would soon face similar situations, with decisions he later might regret. Just like the play, the past was merely visions fabricated with mistakes and memories to grow from. Even though he would never have to worry about getting pregnant, she hoped he would not land on the other side of the situation.

To her left, Sarah's parents sat sharing their own popcorn. Her dad eased his popcorn-free hand over to her mom's, clasping his fingers around her hand. Megan leaned her head over onto his shoulder, giving him a subtle kiss on the cheek. With a marriage of twenty-three years, age was the only piece that changed. Sure, they had their arguments, going the day without talking. Still, no matter what issue crossed their path they always reverted to what she imagined mirrored the time when they first started dating. Maybe that was how they kept the magic alive.

Sarah looked at her brother, who was intently locked on the play, eating popcorn at a stomachache-inducing rate. She decided to give him a nudge, hoping to provoke a scare. He jumped in the seat, and then puzzlingly looked to Sarah for an explanation.

"Do you have any popcorn left?" A disappointed expression clouded his face after inspecting the bottom of the bucket, scattered mainly with hulls and seeds. Matty settled back as her smile confirmed she wanted a laugh, not popcorn.

As the actors gathered at the center of the stage, the curtains were drawn closed. The lights gradually woke the auditorium, announcing the end of the performance. Gathering their belongings and wading through the crowd, her family was greeted at the doors by a shivering burst of wind. The tight clasp of her dress clung close, not able to flutter.

Inspecting the sky, Matty pointed toward a few clouds in the distance. "Do you think it will snow?" he questioned, almost as a plea.

Sarah knew the temperature had not fallen enough for snow or ice, and the lingering clouds held little promise. "Maybe, but if not, that just means you are free from shoveling," she laughed.

The Jeep had long cooled down, but with a few turns of the ignition, the engine sparked to life. Sarah and Matty huddled in the back until the heater warmed up halfway home. The remainder of the ride, Matty was glued to the window, waiting for any sign of snow.

After the Jeep fluttered into the garage, Megan went inside to put on a pot of coffee while the others toted logs inside to rekindle the embers in the fireplace. Cliff poked the fire while Matty and Sarah sat on the floor to watch.

Within a few minutes, the blaze started to crackle and pop. "Coffee is ready," said Megan. Sarah lifted herself from the floor and went into the kitchen.

With each hand steady and cups filled to the brim, they shut off the lights and made a circle in the living room. "Two coffees black, two eggnogs chilled," announced Sarah as she handed Matty his glass.

When the fire's initial flicker became a steady burn and the cups emptied, the four of them gathered around for one last to do before going to bed. Sarah went to the storage closet and pulled out a rather small box imprinted with snowflakes. She lifted the lid, carefully removing the star before handing it to her dad. Cliff always put the star on top of the tree on Christmas Eve. He said it was something his mother and grandmother had taught him.

With the star set aloft at the apex of the tree, glimmers of light reflected from the metal, casting a shimmer about the room. "Alright, Matty and Sarah. Off to bed, you two."

"Dad, you know I can't sleep on Christmas Eve. I am too excited," Matty said.

"Come on, Matty, you can stay with me tonight. I will probably have trouble sleeping, so we can talk if we are both up," Sarah laughed.

"Alright!" he yelled as he raced upstairs.

As she reached the top of the staircase, the light from beneath her door confirmed Matty had already changed into his pajamas and was likely bouncing up and down on her bed. Sarah pulled her pajamas from the dresser and went to the bathroom to change, leaving her brother dancing and singing.

As she finished brushing her teeth, Sarah noticed the room had grown quiet. Opening the door slowly not to wake him, she grimaced at seeing Matty examining her iron pills, anticipating his numerous questions, or worse, digging deeper. She speedily dove across to bed to snatch them.

"What are those?" Matty inquired.

"They are just vitamins," she said.

"What kind of vitamins?"

"You ask a lot of questions, kiddo."

"Can I have one?"

"No, they are for women, not children." She could tell her answer upset him. "Coach told us to take them to ensure we have the right …."

"Can you read me *'Twas The Night Before Christmas?*" he asked, losing interest in details. The book was purposed more as a decoration, but she picked it up and lay down beside her brother anyway. He fluffed the side pillow and snuggled close to her. He was perfectly capable of reading, but she didn't mind.

Only when reaching the proclamation "and to all a good night," did Sarah's voice fade to a whisper. Matty's excitement about Christmas had been overthrown by exhaustion. She slid from the bed to switch off the lights. Feeling her way back, she looked over at the clock. It was eleven thirty. Soon it would be Christmas Day. She nestled up to her brother with her back toward him and drifted off to sleep.

An overwhelming sense of joy jolted Sarah to reality.

"Wake up, Sarah! Wake up!" Her eyes sprang open, startled. She recalled no dreams of haunting ghosts spooking her during the night, nor did any life-altering visions grace her subconscious. Instead of being disappointed in her once-desired fantasy, her drowsy state was replaced with excitement. *Was the excitement from the lack of dreams, or Matty's attack?*

Five thirty, she felt, was too early, knowing they could not venture downstairs unless her parents were awake.

"I'm up, Matty," she gasped as he continued trampolining beside her.

"Are Mom and Dad?"

"Let me go see, but you stay here," Sarah said as she left the room, shutting the door behind her. Barely stepping across the hall to the staircase, she could hear voices carrying from downstairs.

"Matty is ready for presents. Is that alright?" she called.

"Send him down," yelled Cliff.

As Sarah approached the guarded door, Matty's restraint lapsed. He snatched her hand in passing, insisting she not miss the action. She chased after him, skirting down the stairs to where Cliff and Megan sat drinking coffee. Matty wasted no time latching his hands onto the first present. Sarah watched in amusement. Their parents allowed him to thrash away at the paper a few minutes before intervening.

"Here, let's pass them out." Matty quickly switched modes and began reading tags and shuffling the boxes into piles.

"You can open all yours first, Matty," said Sarah after they had sorted everything. He either heard her or paid no attention, for he kept his focus centered on his gifts.

The whirlwind only ceased as he finished tearing all the wrapping from the boxes and commenced playing with his toys.

"Okay, Sarah; you're next." She started with the smaller boxes and worked her way to the largest one. Each gift opened to the thrill of new clothes, a pair of dress shoes, and even a plush coat. When she set aside the last of the paper, Sarah settled into the coat as if snuggling in a blanket while her parents opened their presents.

When all the wrapping paper had been torn and scattered about, the morning sun peeked its way into the living room. Astonishingly, year after year they woke up unreasonably early on Christmas to exchange presents and required a nap by sunrise.

"I think I could lie here all day," Sarah said as she fell back into the couch.

She closed her eyes in the hopes of sleep when a knock came at the door. *That's odd, Grandma and Grandpa usually don't come over until closer to time for church*, she thought. Nonetheless, she stood up to answer the door. "Who is it?" she asked. There was no answer, yet intrigued, she turned the knob.

Perched in a wheelchair, accompanied by her parents, sat a young woman. The blue fingernails only confirmed the masked face marked with scratches and bruises. *Emily*. Sarah's face flushed as she fumbled for words.

Regaining her breathing, she quoth, "Emily? I thought… They said…" Emily began to nod and they both teared up. "How is this possible?"

Emily smiled up at her. "My vitals began to improve, and the next thing I remember was waking up with everyone standing around me."

"Do you remember anything?"

"The wreck feels like a bad dream that I barely recall, and then I just went into a peaceful sleep."

"But what, or how?"

"The doctors claim this has happened before, but it's nothing short of a miracle," Emily replied. "The hospital discharged me with a list of restrictions. I'll have therapy for the foreseeable future and routine exams so they can keep an eye on my progress. When my parents asked me what I wanted to do for Christmas, I said 'I have to go see Sarah.'"

Sarah leaned down to give her a hug, whispering, "I am so sorry, Emily, for everything."

"It's alright, Sarah. I'm sorry too."

"Do they expect for you to make a full recovery?" asked Sarah hopefully.

"Yes and no," stammered Emily. "As far as everyday life, time will tell, but … they are not sure about how well my mobility will develop, or if running is a possibility."

"You will have to, Emm. Otherwise, I will feel bad for eating all the time in front of you," Sarah teased, provoking a laugh.

"Come in. I know my parents will be glad to see you," Sarah continued.

Carter rocked the wheels to pivot Emily over the threshold.

"Mom, Dad, look!" Matty rushed to the door to experience the excitement firsthand. Cliff and Megan followed behind without urgency. Sarah's eagerness dwindled as she noticed the lack of surprise on their faces. "Wait…. Did y'all know?"

"They called last night asking if they could come this morning. I would have told you, but Emily insisted it be a surprise," Megan said.

Cora offered Sarah a hug in consideration for hiding the news.

"And, Sarah, I'm delighted to see you are doing well after your incident."

The words soured in Sarah's stomach as she released her clinch on Cora, but she continued as Sarah pulled away. "We were worried the fainting…." Sarah's horror-stricken face brought the demise to her words.

"Sarah… What is she talking about?" said Cliff.

Sarah turned to embrace the concerned eyes of her parents. She lowered her eyes to the floor. Months of lies and deceit cornered her for the truth.

"Liv, what happened? Is something wrong? How did…" Megan failed to form another word as she waited for Sarah to answer.

She peered up at her parents. Megan's tear-streaked cheeks and Cliff's worried eyes begged for an explanation.

"Sarah, I'm so sorry; I thought they knew," said Cora, placing a soft hand on her shoulder.

"No, it's alright," she said moving closer to her parents. "During the regional race, I blacked out just before the finish. Another girl, Emily, and I were all bearing down the last fifty meters. The last thing I remembered was my body going limp. When I woke up in the hospital, they confirmed I was severely anemic."

"Liv, why didn't you tell us?" Her mother cried as Cliff tried to suppress his anger in coming to grips that his daughter had been hiding something from them. Before he spoke, Cliff exhaled the breath he held.

"Sarah, I think it is best we discuss this tomorrow. Today is Christmas, and seeing that you and Emily are both alright, we need not harp on this now."

Megan sank her head into her hands, sobbing. Guilt still lay heavy on Sarah, knowing she only acknowledged part of the situation. She wanted to console her mother, but even as they hugged, pain struck her own heart.

Cliff reached his hand out to Carter, "Please join us for breakfast. We all could use some coffee, I'm sure." Following the others, Sarah wheeled Emily to the table as Megan retreated to the kitchen to pull a breakfast casserole from the oven and Cliff poured the coffee.

Guilt tugged at Sarah for the remainder of the day. As her grandparents arrived later that morning to join them for church, Sarah longed to be alone. Not from shame, but she wanted time to think. Telling her mom about the pregnancy debacle scared her to the core, but she was upset and needed someone to talk to. Despite everything, admitting the completeness would bring shame, but the hope to relieve the burden weighed greater.

Opportunity knocked that night as she folded down the covers on her bed.

"Sarah?" her mom said, cracking the door open.

"Come in."

"Look, Sarah, I know…" Megan began.

"Mom, wait; there is something else I need to tell you. Just promise me you will still love me."

"Ah, Liv; nothing will ever change that. I know I might be upset, but you will always be my little girl."

Sitting down together on the edge of the bed, Sarah cleared her throat.

"Mom, I don't know where to begin with everything that happened this semester. I made some terrible decisions and well there was this guy I started seeing."

Her mom took her hand and looked into her eyes. She struggled for the next words to say. "I… Well we…"

Megan stopped her. "Are you?" she asked.

"No. We didn't go that far."

CHAPTER 23:

Then Next Semester

The rain beating upon Sarah's window broke the silence of the room. Interrupting her dream, the noise drew her from a tantalizing sleep. She hadn't slept so soundly in months. As the pattering drops grew louder, Sarah rolled over on her side and opened her eyes. Feeling the monthly cramps, she knew it would be another one of those days. A shower and change would be the first things before getting ready for class.

Sliding her legs over the flannel sheets, Sarah Olivia felt her way to the edge of the bed and placed her feet on the soft rug below. The brown strains of hair fell toward the top of her shoulders, almost the right length to cover her neck and meet the seam of her T-shirt. Sarah shut the door to the bathroom behind her and slowly shed the flannel boxers, revealing her firm legs that stretched to her slender waist. The purple panties were the usual, in case of a leak. Clasping at the hem, Sarah pulled the oversized shirt over her head, unveiling her plump breasts. She had never slept in a bra. The thought of being confined by such support seemed unnecessary.

Being free and comfortable was the most gratifying feeling, even if it was just at night. Sarah stood in front of the mirror for some time admiring her body, legs like spun silk, matched with petite hips and ample breasts. However, the reflection she saw in the mirror had changed, in a way that only she knew. Turning the shower handle, she tested the water before stepping inside and drawing the curtain behind her.

After refreshing herself, Sarah slipped into some dark red undies and a pair of fitting jeans. Finally, she strapped on a bra with a cami and long-sleeve blouse. She peered again into the mirror. She felt cute. Of course, she needed to feel satisfied and confident. The rest of the week was going to be a painful few days. Before creeping out the door, Sarah poured a cup of coffee and popped two aspirins. The first day of the semester was here, and hopefully a new start. Putting on her jacket, Sarah opened the door and quietly stepped out into the rain ….

Acknowledgements

I would like to give a special thanks to everyone that helped me along my journey to create this book: My grandparents and parents, for their prayers and keeping the way to pass down to me. My mom, for her patience and work designing the cover. My dad, for teaching me to think outside the box. My sisters, for always pushing me to be better. My sisters and my Coach, for reading the early draft and giving me much needed feedback. Darcy and everyone else that helped with the publishing of this book. Allison, for your kindness and help. My alma mater, for their continued support and friendships. And everyone else that has been a part of my life, thank you. Without you, I would not have ever been able to grow into the person I am today. For that, I am truly grateful.

God Bless,

C.S. McKinney